You Gave Me Wings

Book One in Isabella's Story

Written by

Tinthia Clemant

You Gave Me Wings
By Tinthia Clemant

Published by River Lady Press
riverladypress.com

First Print Edition

Editing by alyssakressbookediting.com
Cover design and formatting by coversbykaren.com

ISBN 978-0-9974371-3-3

For Franny and Harry.
You taught me true love is real.
Blessed be.

I thought writing my second book would be a piece of cake. You Gave Me Wings proved how wrong I was. Isabella's journey took detours, hit roadblocks, and, more than once, sailed off the edge of a cliff. Her story is finished, though, thanks to her having a mind of her own. I'm learning to listen to my characters—they know what's best, as do the wise women who supported this novel. Please indulge me as I thank a few of them. Brandy, without you Isabella would still be suffering from paralyzing fear. Alyssa, your feedback pushed me to create the story Isabella wanted all along. Author Jocelyn Babcock, thank you for your positive influence—blessed be.

I'd also like to thank the folks on Scribophile who spent many hours offering critiques, and my assorted beta readers. Blessings to you all.

One more thank-you, please. To all my fans, grazie. Without you, my words would never have wings.

That's it! Now snuggle down and enter Isabella's world. And tell her I said ciao!

Tinthia Clemant, 2016

You Gave Me Wings

Book One in Isabella's Story

Just when the caterpillar thought its life was over,
it became a butterfly.

Proverb

Prologue

It all started with the box.

One

ECHOES followed Isabella's footsteps. She moved through the rooms of the house where she'd spent her forty-nine years of life. The ghosts of her parents remained silent. She knew they would. They hadn't talked much when flesh and bones, so why would they start now?

She entered the room which until two days ago had been her bedroom. Using the toe of her sneaker, Isabella traced a black line in the aged floorboard. She never should have lit that cigarette. It had been foolish to think her father wouldn't notice the odor. She'd long accepted her stupidity hadn't caused his stroke. However, back then, at age fourteen, she hadn't known any better.

Isabella walked out of the room. She followed the hallway and paused at the doorway of the large front room—her parent's bedroom. Why she still thought of it as their room was beyond her. For three decades her mother had slept in there alone.

Her mother's perfume lingered. Even in the throes of illness, Christina Martini had insisted on a daily bath and a dousing of *Wind Song*. Now, five years past her death, the heady fragrance managed to endure. The new owners would have to strip the walls or fumigate.

A low snicker passed through Isabella's nose. Who was she kidding? The house's days were numbered. When she returned, it would be a gaping hole.

A sigh and shrug followed. Maybe both their days were numbered.

Isabella entered the kitchen. She stood in the spot which, until three days ago, the dinette set had occupied. Her fingers could still feel the cool Formica surface, and her mind's eye saw the color—egg-yolk yellow. Four vinyl-padded chairs had hugged the chrome edging of the table, each seat upholstered in the same horrid color.

Funny how the distance of age changed a person's perspective.

When she had been young, she'd bitched and moaned about the furniture, even going so far as refusing to invite friends over to the house, the shabbiness of the furnishings offered as the reason. While her friends' parents upgraded their nineteen-fifties-styled furniture, Isabella's mother had refused, her middle-class upbringing offered as the reason for holding fast to items long past their lifespans.

Back then, it had been easy to blame her teenage angst on her mother. But the years had brought some clarity. If she could go back, she would shake her young counterpart and tell her to look deeper before it became too late. She would force her sixteen-year-old self to see the truth—it had nothing to do with things; refusing to engage with others centered from her insecurities.

Isabella opened the door and walked onto the back porch. She let her mind drift to the last time she had spoken to her mother. That strange summer day, five years ago.

A distraught caretaker had met her at the door. "Get in the kitchen quick. You won't believe what's going on. She's like her old self. Been like this all day!"

Isabella pulled herself back to the present. Despite the eighty-degree July weather, she couldn't ignore the goosebumps prickling her skin. The memory of seeing her mother seated at the kitchen table chilled her to this day. Travel brochures had littered the table's sparkling surface. She could still see the tentative steps she had taken as she moved toward her coherent mother.

"Ma, what's going on?"

"Hi, darling. How was work? I'm going to Italy. Oh, and I went to the hair salon." Frail fingers patted curls of white hair. "Do you like it?"

"Yes, Ma. I love it. But I don't understand. How do you feel?"

Unsure how a woman went from drooling onto her sweater to planning an intercontinental trip, she had eased a chair away from the table and sat, half listening to the caretaker's ranting. "You should have seen her this morning. Ate six eggs, four slices of bacon, and a full glass of orange juice. Started talking about planning her trip to

Italy. Demanded a visit to the salon. After that, she insisted on visiting the travel agent where she got all them brochures. The only time the dementia returns is when she starts talking about some book and insisting she already has a plane ticket."

"You want to go to Italy, Ma?"

Her mother's brown eyes glossed over as she nodded. "I have a plane ticket, but I can't seem to remember where I put it. And I want my book." A look of overwhelming panic filled had filled the brown eyes. "I need to find the box. Do you know where I put it? I must get to Italy. I must."

"See," the nurse blurted. "She does that. Talks like she's got all her marbles, then slips back into the dementia."

A dampness crept into Isabella's bones as she stood now on the back porch. She played with the wedding band on her right ring finger, her mother's final, haunting words fresh as if they had been spoken yesterday. 'I never regretted my decision, Isabella. Never doubt that.'

The doctor had explained it was common for people suffering from dementia to become intelligible from time to time. As to her mother's death during the night—natural causes was the only explanation he could offer.

Isabella rubbed her arms and turned back for the house. There were so many riddles that needed answering, she didn't know where to start.

She glanced around the kitchen and brought her eyes up to the square opening in the ceiling. She could still see Craig's sweaty face peering down through the hole. What if she hadn't hired him to fix the wiring?

No—she refused to play the 'what if' game. She had hired him and that's what she needed to focus on, along with all the other issues stuffed into her emotional basket.

The beep of a car horn pulled Isabella from her reverie. Her luggage was on the front stoop. She was ready to move on.

In a loud whisper she said, "Goodbye, house. It's been fun, but I've got places to go, sunflowers to count, and a life to save."

After she walked out the front door, Isabella bent and picked a wild rose blossom from the front garden. She placed it on the bottom step and murmured, "Wish me luck, Ma."

Without casting a final glance at the house, she pushed back a tear and walked toward the older man waiting for her by the Mercedes.

"Hi, Carl. Thanks again for driving me," Isabella offered as she walked up to Carl Salzburg, the husband of her friend, Bethany.

Carl lifted the lid to the trunk and inserted Isabella's luggage. "Get ready. She's chomping at the bit."

Although Isabella had assured her friend she didn't mind taking the bus into Boston, Beth had insisted. 'It will give us a chance to discuss any last-minute details.'

Isabella understood the implication of Beth's statement. The ride would give her another chance to try and derail Isabella's trip.

After giving Carl a quick hug, Isabella snickered. "I'm sure. Can we stop for a coffee? And some Valium?"

Carl chuckled. "The coffee I can do."

As she climbed in the back of the Mercedes, Isabella steeled herself for what promised to be a two-hour sermon.

Beth didn't even wait for Isabella to close the door. "Isabella, this is a big mistake."

"Hello to you too. Thanks again for taking me to the airport."

Beth sniffed while frowning. "What else would I be doing, except maybe having my roots colored? They'll have to wait. I'll just explain to everyone we drove you on a fool's errand and I missed my hair appointment. Do you have your passport?"

"Yes, Mom, I do." Isabella kept her voice light. "And I have a dime in case I need to make a phone call."

"At least that comment shows your age if your actions don't. Do you have your cell phone charger?"

"Yes." Isabella gritted her teeth. "I have about a hundred stored in one of my suitcases. Thank you, by the way, for buying them."

"Well, it's the least I could do. Since you're not thinking about your safety, I have to." Beth swung her attention to her husband. "Where are you going, Carl?"

"Isabella wants coffee," Carl responded in a weak voice.

"Thanks for throwing me under the bus, Carl." Isabella chuckled.

Beth turned in her seat. "We don't have time for coffee. Your flight leaves at four, and it's already ten." She faced Carl and added, "Just get going and she can get coffee at the airport."

Carl started to speak, but Beth cut him off. "Carl, just drive. I'm talking to Isabella."

Isabella turned to the window and focused on the passing trees. If she got to Boston without losing her sanity, flying to Italy would be a piece of cake. Cake. Yes. She would order tiramisu on the plane.

Beth adjusted her body to allow her full access to Isabella. "Did you put clean underwear in your carry-on bag? What about your Spanx? Are you wearing them?"

"No. I don't have on the Spanx. I'll be on a plane. Who's going to pinch my ass on a plane? Besides, women getting pinched in Italy is a fallacy."

"American women get pinched. Put on your Spanx when you get to the airport. Your skin will be harder to grab. And don't talk to anyone."

Isabella rolled her eyes and sighed. "Who's going to bother a woman with a bird's nest on her head?"

"Your hair is fine. It was a smart move getting a perm. You got to leave your hair dryer at home, which is one less thing for the airline to lose."

"Have you seen this hair?" Isabella pulled a strand of parched brown frizz."This isn't a perm—it's a burn. There should be tweeting coming from my hair."

"Forget your hair. Is the American consulate's number programmed into your phone?"

"Yes, and I've written it on my arm and thigh just in case I lose my phone."

Carl's chuckle earned him a glare from Beth before she returned her attention to Isabella. "Joke all you want, but I told you this trip is foolhardy. Carl thinks so too. Don't you, Carl? A woman traveling alone in a foreign country. For a month!"

Beth issued another sniff, her face tight with impatience. "You didn't even think this through. You found the box, and the next thing I know you're flying to Italy. This is out of character for you, Isabella. You don't do things like this."

"Well, maybe it's time for me to start." Isabella clenched her hands. "What do I have in New Boston? Truly, what?"

"You have your new house. Think of all the friends you'll make. Living in an adult community will be fun. You might even meet some nice older widower."

"I don't want to make friends in the Gales." Isabella's fingernails dug into her palms. "Plus, I'm forty-nine. I don't want to meet a nice older widower. I want to live. I want to experience life. I want to drink—"

"Is this about Freddy?" Beth cut in.

Isabella rolled her eyes. Why hadn't she taken the bus? "No, this isn't about Freddy. Why do you always think everything is about Freddy? He's been out of my life for years."

"Yes, but he broke your heart. You've never gotten over him. You don't even go on dates."

"Hello… perhaps you've forgotten that I've been taking care of my mother."

"You still miss her?" Beth's mouth set into a firm line. "She died five years ago."

"Of course I still miss her. She was my mother!" Isabella fumbled in her carry-on bag. She was letting Beth pull her into another one of those conversations where she wanted to fling herself off Mt. McKinley.

"What are you looking for?"

"I'm getting a headache. I need some ibuprofen."

Beth nodded. "See, it's this trip. What I don't get is why Italy? You could spend some time in Vermont."

Isabella riffled through the contents of her bag. She needed the pills. Where were they? "Come on, Beth. We've discussed this. I want to see Italy. What's the big deal? Lots of people travel to Italy."

"You're not lots of people. You live a reclusive life. You're a hermit."

Isabella pulled the bottle out and tried to line up the raised, white arrows while keeping her hands from shaking. "I'm not a hermit!"

With more force than necessary, she popped the cap. Pills rained down like confetti.

Isabella threw the empty bottle into her bag and slumped against the seat's back cushion. No coffee. No pills. She needed chocolate.

Beth waved her hand and blocked a pill aiming for her forehead. "You've never even been out of New England, let alone on a plane. Flying is difficult. Right, Carl? We know. We've traveled. You don't even take bus trips. This is all because you found that damn ticket. I should have torn it up when you showed it to me."

Isabella stared over the car's hood at the vehicles ahead of theirs and wrenched at the ring. No matter how many times she explained her reasons, she couldn't get Beth to understand New Boston had become a vacuum and the last bit of air left in her lungs would soon vanish.

"Are you listening to me?" Beth's voice pierced Isabella's ears. "You can't solve your mother's mystery. She's dead."

Isabella stared at Beth. "I'm not trying to solve my mother's mystery. Can't you just be my friend and wish me luck? Be here for me if I fail or celebrate with me if I succeed?"

"Fine." Beth faced the front of the car and fiddled with the radio.

"Thank you."

Isabella remained unconvinced Beth would let the subject drop, but a few moments of peace were better than none.

Kenny G's alto sax lulled her into herself. She slid the gold loop on and off her finger. She wasn't being fair to Beth. With a ten-year difference in their ages, it was no wonder each woman saw life through different eyes. She saw a last chance for a fresh start, while Beth saw life as over.

Beth faced the rear of the car again. "I have one more thing to say, and I'll drop the subject. You've always been a reserved woman,

Isabella. Remember when Freddy would have to go to parties at the law firm? You told me you would sit along the side of the room while he schmoozed. You're not gregarious, you're not outgoing, you're not a risk-taker, and you're not brave."

Beth leaned forward, her head halfway between the front and rear seats. "I wish I knew what you're trying to prove."

Isabella snickered as Beth added, "That's all I'm going to say of the matter." Without waiting for a reply, Beth turned forward again and increased the radio's volume. All talking ended as the sounds of smooth jazz filled the silence.

The car neared the airport. A plane took off in the distance, and Isabella watched its ascent. It wasn't too late to change her mind. Her life was good, as lives went. She could still tell Carl to turn the car around, and spend the night in her prefabricated, Crackerbox-style house. Maybe meeting an older widower would work. She could take care of him, just as she had taken care of her mother. Perhaps that was her path—always to care for someone else instead of herself.

Carl pulled along the curb for Terminal E. Isabella remained in her seat and stared out the window.

Beth turned to face her. "This is it! Are you going or staying? We don't have all day."

"I..." Isabella continued to focus on the world outside the car. If she returned home, she could try again another time, when she was better prepared. What did it matter that she felt strangled by her life? Lots of people felt the same way. Yet, as Beth had recently pointed out, she wasn't lots of people.

"I'm going." Isabella pushed open the car door, then met Carl at the trunk. She took hold of her luggage and walked toward the check-in kiosk.

Beth sprang from the car and stormed forward. "Don't check in here. They'll lose your suitcases."

Isabella handed her ticket to the attendant while offering an apologetic smile. She then turned to face Beth. "Thanks for your concern. They're not going to lose my luggage. Now, give me a hug. I'll call you when I reach Rome. *Ciao*."

"Fine, but don't call me in tears when everything you own is gone." Beth turned away and climbed back into the car. "Come on, Carl, let's go," she shouted out the window.

"For what it's worth, I think you're a helluva brave woman." Carl pulled Isabella into a bear hug of an embrace. "Go get 'em."

"Thank you, Carl," Isabella said. If only his kind words could mend her fractured nerves.

Long after the Salzburg's car receded into the distance, Isabella remained on the sidewalk. The enormity of what she was about to do was starting to feel impossible. *Was* she being foolhardy? There were other ways to restart a life. She could take pottery classes or learn to swing dance. She should go home right now.

Unzipping one of the outer pockets of her carry-on, Isabella pulled out her cell phone. She tapped the screen and lowered her thumb toward Beth's picture.

The tightening in her throat began to close her windpipe. Travelers jostled her. Some grumbled, others bumped and pushed—telling her to move. Only when a woman barked for her to get-out-of-the-way did Isabella set her mouth into a firm line.

Get-out-of-the-way? Absolutely not. She'd been getting-out-of-the-way for far too long, always stepping aside to allow people, and life, to pass by.

Returning the phone to the pocket, Isabella adjusted the bag's strap, straightened her shoulders, then entered the terminal.

It was time to stop getting-out-of-the-way.

Two

ISABELLA smiled at the stern-looking TSA guard. What little confidence she'd mustered while riding up the escalator had evaporated as she neared the checkpoint.

"I put on a sport bra, so I shouldn't beep," she blubbered. "And I'm not wearing a belt or any jewelry, except my ring and my watch. Should I take them off?"

In response to her question, Isabella received a stern, monotone demand to remove her shoes and put them, along with all loose items, into the bins.

Doing as instructed, she placed her bag on top of her sneakers.

"Carry-on goes in a separate bin," the guard barked.

The robot on the opposite side shouted for her to keep moving, collect her things, step aside, and have a nice flight.

"Good thing I'm not wearing a prosthetic leg," she kidded as she walked through the scanner.

The guard repeated his command with rote, monotone efficiency. Had he pulled out a cattle prod, she wouldn't have been surprised.

Isabella fumbled to collect her belongings. Her nerves were firing on all cylinders. Hopefully, Italian security would be less demanding. But would they speak English? What would she do if they didn't? She had two Italian phrases memorized. Unless they said 'thank you very much' or 'have a nice day,' she would be screwed.

"Of course they'll speak English," she muttered. She was just trying to latch onto an excuse to back down. No guts, no glory—right?

She tied her sneakers and looked around. Even with the early boarding privilege Alitalia's first-class ticket provided, an hour of freedom remained. And she still needed coffee. And chocolate.

Isabella joined the crowd and meandered down the concourse. Upon passing a clothing store, an outfit in the shop's window caught her eye. She could see herself dressed in the white capris and yellow top as she walked through the streets of Camaiore. Detouring into the store, she smiled and inquired about her size.

"We have less constricting clothes over by the wall," the young attendant said as she unlocked a dressing room door.

Isabella narrowed her eyes. "Thank you, but I'll be fine." Taking the hangers from the sales girl, she closed the door. This was exactly what she needed—a snarky salesclerk, not even old enough to vote, giving her fashion advice. It was the proverbial cherry on top of Beth's earlier tirade.

As she faced the mirror, the two hangers dangled from her fingers. She gaped at her reflection. It would take more than a pair of capris to fix what she saw.

Who wore linen on an international trip? By the time she arrived at the hotel, her dress would have more folds than an accordion. And the color? What had she been thinking when she purchased the tan shift? With the mop on her head, she resembled a human cigar.

She hung the new clothes on the door and released her bag. It landed on the rug with a heavy thud. She turned her back to the mirror and rested against it. True, she had adopted a conservative appearance, but her clothes were well-made and practical. Muted colors, sensible shoes—a look finely crafted to help her live in the background. So she wasn't a fashion diva. It wasn't as if people would be clamoring to take her picture.

She collected the untouched pants and top and delivered them to the salesclerk.

She didn't need new clothes. The items she'd brought were fine. Functional for the hot, sunny location.

Holding her carry-on bag against her stomach, Isabella exited the store and walked back toward the gate. Maybe the airlines would do her a favor and lose her luggage.

"Hi." Isabella smiled at the older gentleman behind Fuel America's counter. "I'll have an espresso, please. And one of these cupcakes. The one with the chocolate frosting."

"Coming right up," he responded.

After paying, Isabella stepped to the side. The terminal was beginning to fill with travelers, and toward the middle a group started to gather. People waved papers in the air while a security guard stood ground.

"Excuse me, miss, here you go."

The cupcake, along with a cup of coffee, foam swirled to resemble a heart, waited for her on the counter's gleaming surface.

"I love it!" she exclaimed and handed the *barista* a five-dollar tip. "You're an artist."

The man grinned and leaned forward. "You coming or going?"

Isabella took a none-too-subtle step away from the counter. "I'm sorry?"

"The airport. You just arrive or are you catching a flight?"

"Catching, thank you." She removed her food and left. Walking a wide berth around the growing crowd, she found a quiet table near her gate and settled in to finish her wait.

Before taking a sip of coffee, she distractedly ran her fingertip through the curled end of the cupcake's frosting. The taste of the dark chocolate failed to register, her mind still back with the barista. She could have taken up her end of the conversation and asked him about his job. Maybe even flirted a little. Why was that piece of the puzzle so hard to fit? It was like a dance to which she'd never learned the steps. The heart design swirled as she raised the coffee cup to her mouth. She knew the steps. She was just too afraid to rejoin the dance. She might trip and fall again. If she did, this time she might not get back up.

Using a spoon, she scooped more frosting. Licking the white plastic surface, she exhaled a grateful sigh. Good coffee and chocolate. What more could she ask for? If her travels ended here, could she be content? Perhaps she should buy a dozen cupcakes and call Beth and Carl. This time tomorrow she would be behind the walls of her new cookie-cutter house, deep in a sugar coma, totally unaware of her decision to abandon the trip. By the time she resurfaced with a clear head, it would be too late.

In truth, that's what she already feared most—that it was too late.

As the first passenger to arrive, Isabella looked around the empty Magnifica section of the plane and exhaled a grateful sigh. The online diagram had been an exact replica. Five rows of staggered seats lay before her—each row four seats across, starting with a single window seat, a set of double aisle seats, and another individual window seat.

A man with quiet brown eyes greeted her. *"Buonasera, signora.* I am Niccolo," he said in a soft tone, punctuated with a wide smile. "May I have your boarding pass, *per favore*?"

"Hello." Isabella greeted the young attendant. "Of course, here."

After reading her pass, Niccolo nodded and walked over to the first set of double, aisle seats. "*Signora*, your seat is here."

Scrutinizing where Niccolo pointed, Isabella's head pivoted slowly as the corners of her mouth turned down.

The double seats he indicated were called honeymoon seats and angled to allow the occupying passengers to face one another. The inner armrests intimately aligned in such a way that, unless her seatmate's arms were the width of a stick, she would be fighting for equal usage.

"Excuse me. There's been some mistake. I chose a window seat."

"*Si, signora.* However, a change has been made." Niccolo pointed to her newly printed pass. "See, she say here, seat 1G."

Isabella sucked in a breath and pursed her lips. "I don't care what it says there." She pointed to the side. "There. 1J. That was my original choice. I selected that window seat." Her voice shook. "I want that window seat. Or any window seat. I need a window seat."

Niccolo stood steady. "*Scusa, signora*, we cannot alter the arrangement."

"But you did alter the arrangement." Isabella's brows knotted. "You very much altered the arrangement."

Niccolo glanced at the line of passengers waiting to board. He removed a package from seat 1G. "Signora, I am sorry for the inconvenience. You will be comfortable, si." He bent and opened a small cabinet near the floor. "This closet, she is for your suitcase."

"I don't care. I—"

"*Signora*, you will be happy. I will take good care of you. Now, I must help other guests. I will return." Niccolo handed Isabella the plastic bag containing her blanket and pillow. A curt nod followed before he turned and darted away.

Isabella shoved her carry-on into the cabinet, closing the door with a kick of her foot. She dropped into her new seat. If she wasn't so annoyed, she might actually enjoy the feel of the supple Italian leather in which she sank. Unfortunately, if she had been sitting on a throne of rose petals, it wouldn't have mattered—they'd switched her seat.

She buckled her seat belt. Maybe the seat switch was an omen—telling her to abandon ship before she crashed into an iceberg. As Beth liked to remind her, she hadn't thought her decision through.

Perhaps traveling to Italy had been a foolish decision. One month ago she was preparing to move into a new house. Now, she sat on a large airplane, about to fly across two oceans. What if she got shot? Kidnapped? Broke her neck running through a field of sunflowers?

She pressed against the buckle. The cool metal edges dug into her fingers. She couldn't keep waffling. She had to make a decision and stick with it.

With a quick flick of her finger, the buckle popped open. She leaned over and yanked her bag from the compartment, then crammed it back into the cabinet, the door slamming with finality. She'd already wasted a lot of years—what was one more month? Besides, what was the worst that could happen? She'd never actually read of anyone tripping over a sunflower.

Three

A FAMILY of five walked along the opposite aisle. Four children followed a woman like a row of ducklings. Isabella leaned back and watched. Perhaps her seatmate would be someone interesting. A mystery author, heading to Italy to conduct research. Or a teacher.

Niccolo entered the cabin with an elderly woman linked to his arm.

Isabella's spirits lifted. Perfect. She could tell by the way the woman smiled they would enjoy each other's company.

A white-haired man followed behind, dashing her anticipation on the tarmac. It didn't matter. She would try and make the best of the situation.

Niccolo stopped alongside her seat. "*Signora*, you are happy?"

"Yes." Isabella forced a smile and nodded. "Perfect. Great. All good."

"May I offer you refreshment?" he asked.

"Yes. Sparkling water with lemon would be great." Isabella's head bobbed and nodded like a wobble-head doll on a dashboard. "Wonderful. Great."

"They told me the frigging seats would fit me. Whoever thought Asians could build a plane were stupid."

Isabella glanced to her left, her head freezing in mid-nod.

The man resembled a linebacker. Buzzed red hair covered the top of a round head attached to a burly neck attached to a torso sporting thick arms. A Red Sox shirt stretched across his barrel-shaped stomach. Unfortunately, the edge of the shirt and the top of the man's sweatpants barely waved at each other.

"Hey, girlie. Yeah, you. Com'ere." He snapped beefy fingers at a petite, female attendant.

The woman grinned and walked over. "*Signor* Qualdop, my name is Maria. How—"

"Who cares? I want a different seat. This frigging thing is like a vice."

Maria continued to grin. "I apologize, *signor*. We cannot alter the arrangements. *Scuzie*." She turned her back to him and greeted another passenger.

"My stinking company wanted to send me to the plane's frigging back, but I said not on their life. If I have to fly to frigging Italy, I'm riding first class. A fat lot of good it did me." He shouted as he jounced and shifted in his self-proclaimed prison. "Frigging airlines. You're all in cahoots."

As if suddenly realizing someone sat to his right, Qualdop looked over at Isabella. He gave her a once-over with narrow, green eyes. "What's your problem?" the bulbous lips barked.

Isabella stiffened. It was like looking at a car accident. "I... I..."

Niccolo arrived, and she forced herself to watch as he set a bottle, glass of ice cubes, and small dish of lemon wedges on her tray.

She reached for the water bottle and twisted the cap as Qualdop's arms flailed out to the sides. His right hand made direct contact with the open bottle.

Isabella stared down at her saturated lap and then at Qualdop. "Are you kidding me?"

He released a bellyful of beer-tainted breath. "Hey, it's not my fault they make these seats so frigging small. It'll dry. Unless the pilot's an idiot and drops us into the ocean."

The vision slipped in easily. Isabella wiped at her dress a little harder in hopes of blocking the grin that tried to spread across her lips. She clung to a burning piece of wing as Qualdop sank into the frigid, inky waters of the Atlantic.

Qualdop possessed in petulance what he lacked in common courtesy. He flung demands and complaints through the push-back of the plane, while the plane taxied down the runway, during takeoff, and as the pilot set a course for Rome. All in all, by the time the seatbelt light blinked off, Isabella was ready to throw *herself* into the Atlantic.

"Hey, you." Qualdop's elbow shoved Isabella's arm off the joint arm rest. "What's ya' name?"

"You'll have to excuse me." Isabella bent for her carry-on. The flight, thus far, had been smooth, but the slight rocking of the plane forced her to stay rooted after getting to her feet. Using the back of her seat for support, she waited for the uneasy feeling of being suspended in the air to subside, giving Qualdop ample opportunity to offer his comments.

"Going to tinkle?" He released a snort. "There's gonna be a line of people waiting to piss, so don't spend an hour trying to make yourself look pretty. From what I can see, it'll be a lost cause."

Isabella ignored him and faced the aisle. Her original seat had an occupant. The pages of an Italian newspaper blocked his face, but a pair of long legs covered by navy suit pants remained visible. Perhaps he was an Italian aristocrat or villa owner whose private jet was in the shop for repairs. Actually, it didn't matter who he was—he was sitting in her seat.

As she walked by, she noticed the expensive-looking leather loafer encasing a long foot dangling in her direction. A man's foot told many things about other parts of his anatomy. Or so she'd heard. She smiled and chuckled as she approached the restroom. At least she wasn't dead yet. Perhaps there was still hope.

Relieved to see the vacant symbol, Isabella entered the narrow bathroom. She hung her bag on the door. The flight had only begun, yet she felt completely drained. If only she could blink a few times and spirit herself into her hotel room.

Had she known what her seatmate was going to be like, she

would have wrestled Niccolo to the floor of the cabin before submitting to the seating change. Why did she have to have someone obnoxious next to her? On her first flight, too. Did she deserve such a punishment? She was a good person. The kids at school thought so. She didn't assign detentions and always had candy on her desk. She flossed every day and never littered. Why couldn't the elegant Italian have sat next to her? Even a toddler would be better.

"Hey, you," she parodied to the mirror. "What's your name?" Washing her hands, she grumbled, "None of your business."

She pulled her toothbrush and toothpaste out of her carry-on as pounding reverberated through the door. She jumped, sending her toothbrush soaring across the small room where it came to a stop at the base of the toilet.

"Are you kidding me!" she shouted.

She picked up the toothbrush, flung it into the trash, then started to rewash her hands when another boom vibrated along the walls.

Qualdop's voice pierced the door. "Finish up. There's a line."

"Of all the overbearing, puffed-up, moronic asses." The toothpaste tube hit the inside of the sink with a violent slap. "I swear," she seethed. "I might just dump a bottle of water over *his* stinking head."

She knew men like Qualdop. Freddy was one. They were bullies. Freddy, however, had been smoother than the lumbering jerk outside the door. Where Qualdop plowed through people, Freddy oozed charm. It was all the same, though. A bully was still a bully.

Isabella dried her hands. She'd never stood up to Freddy, but she was older now. And tired. Tired of her own disappointment in always backing down. It was time for a personality adjustment. Qualdop deserved his due. And while she was at it, she would give him a large chunk of what she owed Freddy, too.

She flung open the door, her eyes narrowed to piercing slits. "Listen, you—oh!" Her eyelids reversed and popped wide open. "I'm terribly sorry."

At first the slender Asian man looked stunned but soon added a chuckle and grin. "I just got here. The other guy went down there." He pointed to the next cabin. "What a twit."

"You have no idea. Again, I'm sorry for startling you." Isabella stepped past the man. As she walked to her seat, she concentrated on what would have been a poor decision. Really, what had all the fuss been about? So Qualdop was a bully. He was also harmless, as most bullies were. Ultimately, in the end, they move on and find new targets. She just had to be patient.

Isabella had been deep in her thoughts, so it wasn't until she stood at her seat that she heard a man's voice from inside the flight service area. A stream of fluid Italian rode on the rich, baritone sound as male and female laughter followed each string of unintelligible words.

Niccolo pushed a cart from around the wall. His young face wore a wide grin as he chuckled to himself at the private joke. Upon seeing Isabella, his smile broadened. "*Signora.* We will be serving dinner soon." He handed her a warm, damp towel. "I recommend the fish. *Molto bene.*" He kissed his fingertips and then moved down the aisle.

Maria followed with a drink cart. Isabella chose the *Sauvignon doc friuli.* She took hold of the glass, swirled the straw-colored liquid and sniffed. The spiciness of tomato leaves teased her senses. She sipped and held the wine on her tongue, allowing it to excite her taste buds. It was like drinking the sunshine of a Tuscan hill.

As Isabella enjoyed the wine, Qualdop dropped into his seat with enough force to alter the plane's trajectory. He barked for a bottle of beer, bread, and butter. She sighed. Giving the glass a steep angle, she downed the contents. It was going to be a long flight.

"I said they were morons and could keep their order. Just as I thought, I didn't even make it to my car before they came crawling.

That's why I'm number one in sales. I know how to handle people."

Isabella nudged her dinner around the plate. She'd already consumed two glasses of wine. One more and she'd be inebriated, which might not be a bad thing considering Qualdop's blustering.

"My moron of a boss doesn't get how valuable I am. One of these days I'm gonna quit, and his ass'll be up shit creek."

Isabella bit into a piece of cold fish and frowned. She had been looking forward to the salted cod but the coagulated sauce was far from appetizing. Perhaps she should ask for the wine bottle and skip dinner altogether.

"I bet you're from a hick town. You look like you're from a hick town."

Isabella lowered her fork. "Excuse me?" She stared at Qualdop, still not sure she'd heard him correctly. "What?"

"You got cotton in your ears? I said you look like you're from a hick town. Where?"

"New Hampshire. Hick enough for you?" She pushed the plate away and lifted her glass. A small pool of wine remained at the bottom. She arched her head back and willed the drops into her mouth.

"Sheesh, I knew it. Can't stand that place. Full of backwoods yokels."

Isabella looked away. From the corner of her eye, she could make out the Italian's shoe. If she offered him five hundred in cash, would he switch seats?

"You listening?" Qualdop pushed his elbow against her arm.

"I heard you." Isabella said through clenched teeth. "Yokels—got it."

"You been here before?"

"Excuse me?" She couldn't keep the sneer off her lips. "Where? The plane?"

"You slow or something? Here, Italy!"

Isabella stared at Qualdop with stony eyes. "No, I haven't."

"You staying in Rome?"

"Why do you ask?"

Qualdop hooted. "You honestly think I'm interested in you? Jeez, you're old enough to be my grandmother. I'm just trying to be polite."

"Thank you, but there's no need."

"I bet you're traveling alone. Women like you always travel alone. You're a fool. Looking like you do, you'll be dead in a week. Men know a dead weight when they see one, even the ignorant Italians. Give me your number anyway. We can hook up."

"NO!" She couldn't help herself. The word flew with more emphasis than she intended.

If her response offended Qualdop, he didn't let on. "You'll change your mind. Lonely women always do."

Isabella reached for the headphones and slipped them over her ears. If she *were* to respond to his comment, she would say her loneliness had caused her to change her mind about many things. For example, she'd constantly changed her mind about breaking up with Freddy when he would reappear after his long absences. And her loneliness had forced her to change her mind whenever she considered putting her mother in a facility better equipped to care for someone with dementia. She had even changed her mind about keeping her childhood home and now owned a house no bigger than a bread box. She would add that sometimes lonely women don't change their minds, though. Sometimes they learn from the past, let go, and move on. At least, that's what *she* was planning on doing.

She leaned back in her seat. Using the remote control, she increased the volume until the blood in her toes pounded with the strings of Vivaldi's violin concerto.

Like two love-smitten teenagers, the elderly couple seated behind her pressed their heads together as they looked through a magazine.

Isabella began to pass by when the white-haired woman looked up. A smile lit up the woman's creased face.

"Hello," she said and reached out her hand. "It's not my place to say, but you're a saint."

"Excuse me?" Isabella extended her hand and stooped close to hear the soft-spoken voice. "I don't understand."

"Your husband. You're a saint to be married to him."

"Franny, mind your own business." The man arched over the woman's lap. "We're the Carlsons. I'm Harry, and this is Franny, the busybody."

"Oh, Harry, you're such a kidder." Franny released a giggle and planted an affectionate kiss on Harry's cheek before she gave Isabella her full attention again. "He's such a kidder. As I was saying, you're a saint. Your husband—"

Isabella shook her head. "He's not my husband." She crouched next to the seat and lowered her voice. "I don't even know him."

"Well, you're a saint for sitting next to him. What's your name?"

"Isabella."

Franny's brown eyes sparkled under the folds of skin formed from years of living. "Is this your first visit to Italy?"

Harry continued to lean, his hand gently resting on her knee. "Don't mind my wife. She'll talk a blue streak if you let her."

"I don't mind. Yes. It is my first." Isabella set her carry-on bag on the floor. She used it to support her knees and leaned back onto her heels. "What about you two? Have you been before?"

"Oh, yes. We come every year to celebrate our wedding anniversary."

"Why Italy? Did you honeymoon there?"

"We met there," Harry interjected "Twenty-five years ago. Right on the Spanish Steps. My Franny was standing on the steps. Her yellow dress had stains all over the front. She stole my heart." He delivered a loud kiss to Franny's left cheek.

"He's a kidder," she told Isabella. "They weren't all over the front. Just in one spot."

"You met each other in Rome? And then got married! I don't mean to imply… it's… wow!"

"Everyone has the same reaction." Franny giggled.

"The best darn thing that ever happened to me," Harry confessed. "Plus, she's a tiger."

"Oh, Harry!" Franny's cheeks took on a rosy blush. "I'm sorry, Isabella. He's a rascal."

Isabella's spirits soared, and she released a quick burst of laughter—a rare commodity in her life. She had stopped finding reasons to laugh. "I take no offense. I love rascals."

"What about you? Are you married?" Franny asked.

"Me? No." Isabella straightened her legs. "At this point in my life, I can't even imagine falling in love. This trip is taking all the courage I have."

"Miracles do happen, if you believe," Franny stated. "Rome *is* the city of love, you know."

"Aw, you always say that," Harry said. "Paris. *That's* the city of love."

"No, *Rome* is the city of love." Franny turned back to her husband and added, "It's why the movie *Three Coins in a Fountain* was made there."

"I don't care what was made where. Paris is the city of love."

"It was nice meeting you both. If you'll excuse me." Isabella left the Carlsons to their discussion and finished the walk to the restroom.

Four

WHEN she neared her seat, Isabella stopped. Her Italian villa owner leaned against the flight service area's side wall with his back toward her. Tall and broad shouldered, he had a waist that narrowed easily above the long legs. She studied the salt-and-pepper waves of hair curling over the collar of a lavender shirt, neatly tucked into pants that hugged a perfectly formed butt.

"My, my my," she said under her breath. "I am so glad I'm not dead."

A hand tapped Isabella on the wrist.

"He is quite the looker, isn't he?" Franny Carlson added her girlish giggle before asking, "Would you like to sit with me? Harry's visiting with his family for a while."

"I'd love to." Isabella navigated to Harry's vacant seat. "Harry's family is here, you said?"

"Oh, yes. The whole clan is joining us to celebrate our anniversary. Except his son." Franny paused. A slight quiver passed over her lips. "His son never forgave Harry for marrying me. He called me a gold digger."

"I'm so sorry to hear that."

"Oh, it's getting better. He might arrive in time for our anniversary dinner." Franny patted Isabella's hand.

A jolt to her lungs made Isabella gasp. Something about Franny reminded her of her mother. Not the confused woman but the vibrant woman—the woman Christina Martini had been before the illness claimed her. It wasn't the skin tone. Nor was it the voice. Where Franny's was soft and low, her mother's had been lilting and musical. And unlike Franny, her mother had been shy; she would never have started a conversation with a stranger. Honestly, there wasn't anything about Franny remotely similar to her mother. So, where was the familiarity?

She looked down at the hand resting on hers. That was it. That mannerism. Her mother had always held and patted her hand. No matter how bad things got after her father's death, she always knew they would be okay thanks to that simple gesture. That had been the final piece of her mother the dementia had claimed.

"Are you alright? Your hand is suddenly like ice." Franny rubbed the back of Isabella's hand.

Isabella shook off the memory and focused on Franny. "Sorry. I'm a little nervous. This is my first time flying." She forced a smile. "Tell me about you and Harry. How you met and fell in love?"

"Well, I was on vacation with my girlfriend. I had just turned fifty, and we decided to visit Rome."

"Where did you live?"

"Grand Haven, Michigan. A lovely place. I was a nurse, you see. Lizbeth, that was my friend… she's deceased now. She and I were eating our *gelato* when this man walked over to me. He said I was as pretty as a picture, even with the chocolate stain on my dress. Well, I was mortified to look down and see the mess I had made. He laughed and said not to worry; I was still the prettiest woman."

Isabella watched as Franny's eyes took on a far-off look, as if she was wearing her yellow dress and meeting Harry for the first time on the Spanish Steps. "What about the love part?" she asked.

"Harry came to my hotel and took me out to dinner. We spent the next two days together. My girlfriend Lizbeth wasn't happy at all. She's deceased now."

Franny quieted. Isabella watched as sadness passed over her features like a cloud passing in front of the sun. The sparkle in Franny's eyes faded and her lips trembled. Yet, as quickly as the light vanished, it returned and the story continued.

"Let me see. At the end of the vacation, we went our separate ways. Then one day he walked onto the floor where I was working. I was a nurse, you see. I almost fell over. He got down on one knee and said he loved me and wanted to marry me."

"Okay, stop the bus," Isabella exclaimed. "You knew him less than a week, and he proposed marriage? Did you love him?"

"Oh, yes. But I was too shy to say anything. Plus, I was a spinster, you see. I hadn't had many sweethearts. Only one, really. But he was nothing like Harry."

"Did you say yes?"

"Oh, no. I told him to go to his hotel and I would think about it."

Isabella sat on the edge of the seat and stared at Franny. How did two people go from being strangers to falling in love—in such a short amount of time, no less? "So when did you tell him yes?"

"I called him that night."

"And you didn't have any qualms? You were sure?"

Franny laughed. "Oh, no. I was frightened out of my wits."

They both rested their heads against their chairs and giggled like a couple of young girls.

"*Scuzie, signora*s, may I bring you both *espresso*?" Niccolo walked up behind Isabella.

Franny wrinkled her nose. "Oh, none for me, Niccolo. I'll never get to sleep."

Isabella arched her head back and smiled. "I'll take decaf coffee at my seat, *grazie*. And, I'd love to see the dessert cart." She faced Franny and asked, "So what changed? How did you get over the fear?"

"Well, you see." Franny leaned forward and lowered her voice. "Harry was sure. And I trusted him." Her eyes shone. "I knew I could trust him from that first day on the Steps. And I've never been wrong."

The lump in Isabella's throat refused to budge. There was nothing she could say. The beauty of Franny's words made a home in her heart.

A hand rested on Isabella's shoulder. "Mind if I reclaim my wife?"

She turned. "Of course." Leaning forward, she kissed Franny's cheek. "I enjoyed our visit and hope I see you again someday."

Before leaving, she added a peck to Harry's cheek. "Your wife is a dear."

He gave a knowing grin and took over the seat Isabella vacated. She lingered and watched as Franny kissed her fingertips and placed the kiss on Harry's lips. Franny's simple gesture spoke volumes. It had been an expression of love shared by two people who knew each other's road maps—the hills and valleys, the craggy rocks and tangled thorns. It said we'll always be together, despite the distance life may place between us.

Melancholy seeped into her spirits, and by the time Isabella sank into her seat, her thoughts were in turmoil. Had her parents shared that strong a bond? The contents of the box indicated otherwise. If they had, why would her mother have kept secrets?

"It's about time you and the old biddy stopped yammering." Qualdop glared at Isabella, a sour expression on his face. "I have a frigging headache thanks to the two of you."

Still deep in her thoughts, Isabella focused on the glittering band on her finger. She let Qualdop's comment drop into the narrow space between the armrests as she used her left index finger to trace the top surface of the golden loop. What about her? Would she ever find love? And if she did, would she be able to trust him the way Franny had trusted Harry, or would she allow the past to paralyze her?

An unknown quantity of time remained. She couldn't recapture the wasted years. Why try? However, if she could use them as a yardstick to measure the future, she still might be able to conduct CPR on her life. Then maybe, just maybe, she'd find a pulse and start to live.

Niccolo arrived with Isabella's coffee and a shot glass of *amaretto*. She began to say thank you but changed her mind. The time seemed perfect to take a tiny step. If she only used a few Italian phrases, 'thank you very much' needed to be one of them.

"*Grazie mille*, Niccolo."

Niccolo kissed his fingertips. "Ah, *signora*, the flight, she is now good? By the time we land, you will be singing."

Isabella chuckled. She would cut one hell of a figure belting out 'That's Amore" as she skipped off the plane in her crinkled dress, clunky sneakers, and with a bird's nest on her head.

"You a teacher or something?" Qualdop grumbled.

Isabella poured the a*maretto* into her coffee. She stirred the steaming liquid and inhaled the warm aroma. After a long sip, she responded, "I'm a librarian."

"Sheesh, I knew it. You're all mousy and unattractive," he snorted. "You remind me of old Miss Shewster. She—"

Enough was enough. Her voice rang sharp and sudden as Isabella slammed the cup onto her tray. "Mr. Qualdrip, stop talking. Just stop talking. Save your condescending, rude, bombastic comments for someone else!"

"Number one, lady," he shot back. "The name's Qualdop and B, you should be glad a man is giving you any attention. What'd you do, stick your finger in a light socket?"

He looked around the cabin, as if he expected applause. None came, but that didn't stop him. "Another thing. Where'd you get that dress, the—"

"That's it!" Isabella slammed her fist next to the cup and shot him an icy glare. "If you say one more fucking word, I will push your ass off this plane."

"And I'll help her," someone, several rows back, called out.

Qualdop and Isabella remained locked in a staring match until she hissed, "I. Dare. You. To speak."

He turned away as Franny's giggles mixed with the sound of applause.

Isabella stared at the ceiling of the plane. Like an unrelenting battering ram, Qualdop's snores pounded her head. She could almost feel the cabin pressure plummet each time he drew a breath. The earplugs proved useless, and with the pillow held over her head, she couldn't breathe. Short of stuffing a sock in his mouth, she was out of options.

"Screw this," she huffed. After adjusting the chair into its upright position, she turned on her dome light and then bent forward for her bag.

Maria poked her head around the service wall. She walked over to Isabella and smiled. "*Signora*, the sleep she cannot come?"

"No," Isabella chuckled. "The sleep she cannot come." She stood, her five-seven frame towering over the petite attendant. "Do you get to sleep?"

"*Si, signora.* We take the turns. Niccolo, he is resting. May I bring you a refreshment?"

"That would be great. But, please, no coffee. Perhaps decaffeinated tea. And two *biscotti. Grazie mille,* Maria."

"*Prego, signora.*"

Maria retreated while Isabella turned to face the dimly lit cabin and her familiar route to the bathroom. The dome light to her left caught her eye, as did the salt-and-pepper waves reflected in its beam. The handsome villa owner sat immersed in a book.

As Isabella passed, he glanced up. Her right foot remained in mid-step while her jaw swung low. It wasn't possible. She knew the full lower lip, the dimpled chin, and the three perfect creases between the disarming gray eyes. Perhaps she *had* fallen asleep, and this was a dream. If so, she didn't want to wake up.

He cocked an eyebrow and lifted his index finger to his lips, as if to tell her to remain silent. A quick wink followed. Then he crossed his legs and returned his attention to the book, breaking the spell that held her stationary. She sprinted forward and burst into the bathroom. Her bag hit the sink. She pressed her hands against her mouth as a muffled squeal escaped. Scott Hancock was on the plane—and in her original seat!

She reached for the edge of the sink and bent forward, her breaths coming in quick, ragged pants. Her reflected eyes looked ready to pop. For the past four hours, she had been ogling one of Hollywood's sexiest men.

The sex scene from his latest movie looped through her mind. Falling dangerously into the X-rated realm, this one had left very little to the imagination. There was no denying the truth—Scott Hancock had a great butt, along with other, equally great swoon-worthy parts.

Was she brave enough to speak to him? What should she say? Nice ass? The tiny bathroom shrank as she paced its confines. Autograph! She could ask for his autograph. Simple and direct, and it would be something he'd be used to.

"Piece of cake," she told the woman with the wild hair reflected in the mirror. Perhaps she should address her hair first.

Running her hands under the faucet, she wet the parched curls. She mashed them, scrunched them, twirled them, and re-flattened them. It was no use. She *did* look like she had stuck her finger in a light socket.

"Who cares? It's not like I'm going to sleep with him."

Isabella laughed as she fished a notebook and pen from her bag. Imagine if she called Beth to say she'd joined the mile-high club with Scott Hancock. The last time she'd had sex was the same year *Harry Potter and the Sorcerer's Stone* was published. Over the years, Rowling's characters had gotten more action then her, and they weren't even real. Hell, her students were getting more action than her. Everyone was getting more action than her. Once she accomplished her main goals for the trip, she would add sex to the list. First, though, she had to clarify her main goals, but now wasn't the time—she had a handsome actor to approach.

Quietly moving past the sleeping passengers, Isabella looked into the first-class cabin. Her dome light remained the single beam. The giddiness of the previous moments faded. She shrugged and returned to her seat. She'd spent too long fussing over her hair and lack of sex and had missed her chance.

Qualdop's snoring, having decreased to a rhythmic wheeze, supplied the soundtrack to Isabella's thoughts. She sipped the dregs of the cold tea. It was as if she had needed to be forty thousand feet in the air to see the patterns of her life. Her choices boiled down to one thing—fear. She refused to live out loud due to fear. Fear of more losses. Fear of disappointment. Fear of being hurt. Fear of fear.

She didn't get Scott Hancock's autograph. Big deal. What mattered more: trying or succeeding? The fact she was willing to try had to be worth something. And she was here, wasn't she? True, if Craig hadn't found the box, she wouldn't have even planned this trip. Although, she could have replaced the cover, stored the box with the other relics of her past, and ignored the whispers. But she hadn't. She had touched the ticket, slid the ring on her finger, and read the book—events *she* had controlled.

As every gardener knew, to encourage new growth, the dead portions needed to be cut off first. Isabella leaned forward and removed her tablet from her bag. Once connected to the Internet, she searched for a hair salon near the hotel. Better than expected, the hotel hosted its own salon. She programmed the salon's number into her contacts. After the plane landed, she would call and make an appointment. It was time to cut off the dead wood.

Five

WITH the jet bridge firmly fastened in place, Niccolo announced that the passengers of the *Magnifica* cabin could disembark. Eager to depart the confines of the plane, Isabella walked toward the exit. Scott Hancock stood immersed in conversation with Niccolo while the pilot stood to the side of the door.

"*Signora*, I hope your visit to Italy is a pleasant one," the pilot offered as she passed by.

"*Grazie mille*," she said and exited the plane.

She took a few steps but instead of moving forward, she found herself propelled toward the wall. Hitting her shoulder, she angled to see Qualdop's sneer.

"Have a nice trip?" He started to walk away when a loud voice rang out.

"Hey, you." Scott Hancock moved quickly.

Qualdop stopped and turned.

"Yes, you. Apologize to the lady."

Although Hancock's six-three frame towered over him, Qualdop stood his ground. "Mind your own business, you limy ass."

"What? Raised in a bloody barn, were you? I said apologize." Hancock swung the strap of his carry-on off his shoulder and dropped the bag to the floor. "Go on, or I'll have the authorities on you," Scott shouted.

Isabella remained to the side and watched the scene play out, along with half the passengers who were more interested in the tall Brit yelling at the top of his lungs than in entering Italy.

The pilot, accompanied by Niccolo, pushed through the crowd. "*Signor* Hancock, *va tutto bene*?"

"This piece of *merda* shoved this woman." Scott spit out the word *merda*.

From the snicker Niccolo released, Isabella reasoned it had to have been an insult.

"I see," said the pilot. "Perhaps, *Signor* Hancock, you would be kind enough to allow me to handle this."

Scott ran his right hand through his hair and nodded. He lifted his bag and then stood in front of Isabella. "Are you okay?"

Isabella's voice abandoned her. A million ways to start her vacation could have been thrown at her, but she would never have guessed Scott Hancock talking to her as one of them. She stared into gray eyes resembling storm clouds. All she had to do was say 'I'm fine' or 'thank you.' Instead, she nodded and bit the edge of her lip.

"Right. Then I'll take my leave." Scott faced the pilot. "Make him bloody apologize."

Isabella watched as he stormed away with a crowd of people in pursuit, calling out for autographs.

"*Signora*, do you wish to press charges?" The pilot asked.

"What?" Isabella swung her head to face the pilot. "I'm sorry? Oh!" She looked at Qualdop and back to the pilot. "No." She gave her head a shake and waved her hand as if flicking away a bug. "Just let the piece of *merda* go."

In a poor attempt to disguise his laugh, Niccolo covered his mouth and coughed.

"No wonder this stinking country is falling apart," Qualdop spat. "You're all a bunch of frigging morons."

He pushed by the remaining passengers and plodded down the jet bridge.

"*Signora*," the pilot said as he continued to chuckle. "Are you sure?"

Isabella shot a dirty look Qualdop's way before she refocused on the pilot. "I'm fine. Thank you for a wonderful flight."

After speaking briefly with the pilot, Niccolo took Isabella by the elbow. "Come, *signora*. I escort you to passport control."

The ladies' room was packed. Isabella sat in a noisy stall and admired the lone stamp on her passport while she waited for Beth to answer.

"What's wrong?"

She barely heard Beth over the din of flushing toilets and hand dryers.

"Beth, I'm here! I'm in Italy."

"What?" Beth shouted.

"I'm here." Isabella pressed the phone to her ear. "I'm here!"

"Did you get pinched?"

"Forget the pinching. Scott Hancock was on the plane."

"Who? What? I can't hear you." Beth's tone started taking on an impatient tinge. "Where are you?"

Isabella forced the words. "Beth, listen. Scott Hancock was on the plane."

"Who?"

She should have texted. "Scott Hancock!"

"Wait, *the* actor Scott Hancock?"

"Yes."

"On the plane?"

"Yes."

"Did you get his autograph?"

"No." Isabella pressed her free hand to her other ear. "Say that again?"

"Are you wearing your Spanx?" Beth's voice screeched against Isabella's eardrum.

The call ended. *No Signal* flashed on the screen.

Isabella laughed and zipped the phone into its pocket. Only Beth could get from her friend meeting a Hollywood actor to a pair of Spanx.

She reached into the bag's main compartment and pulled out an unopened package. Should she put them on? The plastic slid against the shiny, black undergarment.

"Naw, no one's going to pinch my butt."

On her way out of the bathroom, she deposited the bag into the trash.

It was like trying to find a needle in a haystack. There had to be several hundred people filing down to the baggage claims area. Far more than the two hundred passengers who had been on the Airbus. From her vantage point at the top of the escalator, Isabella surveyed the top of the crowd. What was she thinking? Someone of Hancock's fame wouldn't mingle with tourists. His luggage had probably been hand delivered to a waiting limousine.

She made it to the bottom and moved into the crowd.

"This is going to be a long wait," she mumbled and inched between the bodies. Maybe her luggage would come out first. She just had to get near the carousel.

"Ouch!" She stepped into an older man. "I apologize. Something just—"

The man looked past her and laughed.

Isabella spun around.

A teenage boy wearing a soccer shirt grinned through a thick layer of pimples. His companions, a group of teens wearing similar shirts, laughed as they disappeared into the crowd.

"*Ciao, signora,*" Isabella's assailant called out before he followed his teammates.

"Why, you little…" Isabella rubbed her left butt cheek. The little shit had grabbed a handful of flesh. She would definitely be black and blue.

"Welcome to Rome," she chuckled. "I've officially arrived."

The customs official hadn't asked to look in Isabella's luggage.

She received a friendly grin and wave, indicating she should keep moving. Returning his smile, she passed through the gate.

Before she engaged a minibus tout, she needed a little time to process the past twenty-four hours; she wanted to begin the next phase of her journey with a clean slate. And she needed coffee. And the sudden wave of angry gurgles emanating from her stomach never failed to get her attention. She needed something to eat, too.

It was laughable. For a country mouse, she was about to investigate a second airport. And this one was on foreign soil. She was becoming a cosmopolitan.

Isabella found the perfect spot on the mezzanine. A long, brightly lit pastry case wrapped around the café, and the pungent aroma of freshly ground coffee beans hung in the air. How she planned on carrying coffee while pulling the two suitcases still remained to be seen. If need be, she would hold the cup between her teeth.

"*Buongiorno. Cappuccino. Grazie.* And one of those?" Isabella pointed to a collection of rolls displayed in the case. "*Cornetto marma… arma—*"

The correct pronunciation flowed beautifully out of the *barista's* mouth. "*Cornetto armellata, signora.*"

A stream of Italian flew over her head. "*Avrò lo stesso e sto pagando per entrambi, grazie.*"

She didn't need to turn to know who stood behind her. The look on the *barista's* face confirmed what the heat in her cheeks shouted.

"May I join you?" The deep timbre of Scott Hancock's voice eased itself into her ears.

THE baritone voice, the fluid pronunciation of the Italian words, even the earthy fragrance seeped into Isabella's blood, fueling a firestorm of sparks and weakening the muscles in her body.

Scott leaned his elbow on the counter and angled to see Isabella's face. "Here's a thought. Why don't you find us a table over by that shop and I'll collect our order?"

Without casting an upward glance, she nodded and shuffled away. What had she been about to do? Right, breathe. She had to remember to breathe. Plus, move the cement blocks pretending to be her feet. And what was up with her knee joints refusing to bend? She must resemble Dr. Frankenstein's creation. The only thing missing were the stiff arms and the moans. Thank goodness her arms were busy dragging her luggage—and confidence. As for the moans—it would only be a matter of minutes before they started.

What does a woman from rural New Hampshire say to a famous actor, anyway? How's the hired help? Banged any hot starlets lately? What if she drooled? Snorted? It wasn't as if her body was cooperating. What had she wanted to remember? Something to do with—

"Do you always move so slowly?" Scott came up behind her. "Here, trade." He handed Isabella a tray and took hold of her luggage handles. "Race you."

When she arrived at the table, Scott took hold of the tray, his voice lighthearted. "I feel I could have run through the airport and still gotten here before you."

Isabella looked up. The amusement in the gray eyes sealed her throat as the turbulence outside the plane rocked the cabin. She should sit and fasten her seatbelt. Wait! She wasn't on the plane. So, why was the floor moving?

"I'm nervous," she muttered.

"Nothing to be nervous about. I put my trousers on one leg at a time, just like every other bloke." Scott winked. "I do, however, take them off both legs at a time."

Isabella released a shaky breath. Was it possible to spontaneously combust? If she focused on something other than the man presently holding the back of a chair, she might get through this without finding out.

Scott angled his head and grinned. "Perhaps you should sit before you fall over." He pushed the chair against Isabella's legs, then sat in a second chair and slid one of the cups toward her. "I had the *barista* prepare the *cappuccinos bollente*. I can't stomach lukewarm coffee." He raised his cup forward. "Care to join me?" His grin spread across his face and up to his eyes.

Isabella held the sturdy paper cup with jittery hands. She wanted to drink, but how, without dumping her coffee onto her lap? This wasn't going to be easy.

"Cheers." Scott leaned across the table and tapped his cup against the one Isabella gripped. "By the way, what should I call you?"

Isabella blinked and looked at Scott. "Me?"

"Yes, you. I don't see anyone else here, do you?" Scott pretended to look around. He zeroed in on Isabella again, his gray eyes sweeping across her face before coming to rest on her eyes. "I'm Scott Hancock, but I imagine you know that by now."

Isabella strengthened her hold on the cup. "The movie star."

"Yes, well, let's just go with Scott, shall we? And you?"

"Me?"

"We seem to be caught on a carousel. Yes, you."

"Thank you."

"Your name is thank you?"

"No."

"Your name isn't thank you?"

"Yes. No. Thank you," Isabella blurted. "For what you did...

" Her head jerked backward. Does passing through a time zone cause nerve disorders? It was as if her body systems were failing. What next, her bladder? Would she go into convulsions?

"That tosser needed an attitude adjustment. And, you're welcome…"

"Excuse me?" Isabella managed to lift her cup to her lips.

"I said you're welcome and paused. That was your cue to insert your name. You do have a first name?"

"Yes."

"And?"

"Excuse me?" Her cup remained midair.

"Your first name is excuse me?"

"No."

"Your first name isn't excuse me?"

"No."

Scott released a laugh that started deep in his chest. She knew the laugh. She had heard it during interviews and in movies. Now, here she was, bearing witness to it in real life. Truly, only Woody Allen could write such a comical scene. The small town librarian with the bird's-nest hairdo, and the dashing actor with the mesmerizing eyes. She should email the idea to him.

"I say, you're a hard one to have a conversation with. Do you always answer in one-word responses?"

"No." Isabella shook her head and took a long draw of coffee. "I'm Isabella Martini. And, thank you… for my breakfast."

"My pleasure." Scott pulled off a chunk of *cornetto*. "First trip to *Lo Stivale*?"

"*Lo Stivale?*"

"The boot. Italy."

"Yes." Isabella took another long drink of coffee. The brain fog was dissipating. She sat at a table in Italy's *Leonardo da Vinci* Airport. That much she understood. But she was sitting across from a movie star, and he was attempting to make conversation. That last part was hard to grasp. And posed the million-dollar question.

Isabella set down her cup and clutched her hands under the table. "Why are you here, Mr. Hancock?"

"I'm here to visit my home before heading out for a long shoot. Why are you here, Miss Martini?"

"No, I mean at this table."

"Oh, here, meaning this table. Well, I'm here, at this table, to have a *cappuccino* with you."

"And?"

Scott raised an eyebrow. "I say, perhaps you could string a few more words together to help me out. And, what?" He grinned, the outer corners of his eyes crinkling under its effects.

"I'm sorry." Isabella noted the prickles of sweat beading along her breastbone.

Scott ran his hand through his hair. "You've got me completely bamboozled. Am I supposed to answer or ask?"

"You're Scott Hancock," a sharp voice intruded.

Scott turned and grinned. "Guilty as charged."

A tall woman dressed in a turquoise running suit shoved a book under his nose. "Here." A pen followed. "Write, 'To Maggie, with love, Scott Hancock.' And put the date and time. And sign it."

After Scott complied, the fan stomped away.

Isabella nodded after the woman. "Are all your fans that rude?"

"It's a mixed bag." Scott shrugged and sipped his coffee. "Are you staying in Rome?"

"Yes."

"Ah, yes. Good. I was afraid you might start chattering, and I'd have to hush you. Don't want you running off at the mouth, now, do we?"

"Do you wear contacts?"

Scott laughed and arched forward, his eyes capturing Isabella's. "I have perfect vision. Why?"

"Your eyes. The color. They're gray."

"Yes, so I've been told. My mum had gray eyes. According to my father, that's what first drew him to her."

"Well, they're… arresting."

"As are yours," Scott responded.

She would like to have dropped her gaze, but the steel-colored eyes held tight. "My color is common."

"I disagree. Brown eyes are the true windows into the soul."

Isabella ripped a corner of her *cornetto* and slipped it between her lips and chewed. What was the harm? If she could keep from choking, the banter would be fun. "You're smooth, but I don't believe Powers specified an eye color."

"Ah, true. However, if Hiram was asked an eye color, I'm sure he would have chosen brown." Scott lifted his cup. "And, *touché* for knowing the author."

Isabella tore off another piece of bread. A dollop of filling clung to the edge of her finger. Instead of wiping it with a napkin, she licked the strawberry jam off her skin. What had she been thinking about? Something about choking.

"I have a feeling I'd have better luck if I continued this conversation on my own. However, never say die." Scott's eyes followed her movements.

"I'm sorry?" Isabella gave her head a slight shake before taking hold of her coffee cup.

"Where are you staying?" Scott asked.

"Rome."

"All over or in one particular spot?"

"One spot," Isabella said.

Scott formed a half-grin. "Will you narrow the area or shall I start to guess?"

"I'm staying at the Hassler."

"*Bravo*. Are you able to say it in Italian?"

"Why?"

"Well, it might have something to do with you being in Italy. Give it a go."

She saw the language program's video in her mind. A woman and man stood on a street corner. The conversation flowed, but the subtitles blurred.

"I don't have any idea how to say it in Italian. At the moment, I'm having trouble with English."

Scott leaned against his chair. "I'm staying at the same hotel. May I offer you a lift?"

Isabella raised her cup. Had he just asked to drive her to the hotel? The entire situation was starting to take on a *Twilight Zone* feel. If the ghost of Rod Serling sauntered by, she wouldn't have been the least surprised.

"No offense, Mr. Hancock, but I'm still unclear why you're sitting here. With me."

"Why not you?"

Isabella neither drank nor returned the cup to the table, but held it near her lips. "For one thing, I'm not famous."

"Miss Martini, I do a job. I'm an actor. Nothing more. I'm also a man who reads, enjoys the telly, an occasional bet on the ponies, football, which you would call soccer, a pint now and then, and meeting people." Scott rested his elbows on the table. "If I was a *barista*, would you have a difficult time talking with me? If not, let's pretend I'm a *barista*."

Isabella added a snicker and finished her coffee. She crumpled her napkin and shoved it into the empty cup. "Mr. Hancock, you are not a *barista*. You're famous. You could have a conversation with anyone at this airport. Why me? I'm a plain, simple woman from a small town in New Hampshire."

It was Scott's turn to snicker. "Do you have twenty cats?"

"Excuse me?"

"Well, from your description, you should have cats."

"No," Isabella tore another chunk of bread. "I don't have cats.

I don't even have fish. Although, I did occasionally have a spider or two, but I suspect my new home won't even have those. Just tell me. Why me?"

Scott finished his *cornetto,* wiped his hands, then leaned forward. "Fair enough. I'm intrigued by you. And when I saw you at the counter, I decided to join you. Presumptuous, perhaps." He added a corner of a grin. "However, now I find myself faced with a challenge. And I never back away from a challenge."

"Intrigued by me? I intrigue you? Now, I'm *intrigued.* Alright, I'll bite. How do I intrigue you?"

"Ah, I didn't say intrigue; I said intrigued. However, you become more intriguing with each passing moment."

Isabella drew in a breath. "Fine. I intrigued you. How did I intrigue you?"

"Scott!"

Scott turned his head and sprang from his chair. "Christian!" With a quick movement, he was at the man's side, shaking his hand. "What are you doing here, mate?"

Isabella gawked—now there were two of them. Either she was losing her mind, or the universe was hell-bent on throwing everything it had at her.

With the second actor by his side, Scott returned to the table. "Christian, this is Isabella Martini. Isabella, this is—"

"Yes, I know who this is." Isabella extended a limp hand. "How do you do, Mr. Warner."

"Charmed," Christian Warner said as he placed a lingering kiss on Isabella's palm. His blue eyes remained on her while he asked Scott, "Why is it, Hancock, in a sea of daisies, you managed to find the desert rose?"

Scott clapped him on the shoulder. "Leave Isabella alone. She's not game for your type."

Christian flipped a chair around and straddled it, his broad grin revealing the world-famous dimples.

A new wave of fever inflamed Isabella's cheeks. If only someone would throw water on her. Where was Qualdrip when she needed him? The entire morning wasn't making any sense and the more time passed, the more bizarre it became. She lived in a small town of five thousand people. She knew the butcher by his first name; had been using the same pharmacist for over thirty years; and even shopped at the same grocery store her mother used to take her as a child. How then, did she end up at a table, at an Italian airport no less, with two dashing actors? The entire situation defied logic.

Scott excused himself. Isabella watched him walk across the plaza in the direction of the news shop. He walked with the confidence of a man who knew his place in the world. An older woman turned as he passed. She spun and followed him into the store. Isabella followed Scott's movements among the store's displays. He stopped and spoke to the woman. Although his disarming smile was aimed at the fan's direction, Isabella felt its effects as a shiver tickled her spine.

"Have you known Scott long?" Warner asked.

Isabella refocused on the blond actor. Why was another celebrity speaking to her? Shouldn't he be talking to his agent or something?

"Me?"

"Are you and Scott..." He banged his two index fingers against each other.

"No. No!" Her cheeks stung from the heat building under them. "NO!," she repeated.

"So how do you know him?"

"I just met him. We're not... we were on the same flight but we're not..."

"How did you get from the plane to here?"

"He helped me. That's all. And bought me breakfast."

Scott returned with a newspaper and three bottles of sparkling water.

He removed one of the caps and placed the open bottle in front of Isabella. "You looked as if you might catch fire."

The second bottle he gave to Christian. "Tell me. What are you doing in Italy?"

"I just returned from Florence. Your agent said you'd be landing this morning, and I decided to try and find you."

"Perhaps I should be going." Isabella pushed back from the table.

Christian shook his head. "Don't go. I only need a minute of Scott's time, and then you two can get back to whatever it was you two were about to do."

Scott placed his hand in front of Isabella. "Just give us a moment, would you? Let me have the condensed version, Chris."

Isabella reached for the bottle. While she sipped, she watched the two handsome actors. Warner's golden California looks contrasted with Scott's dark, rugged features. The three creases between Scott's brows gave his face character while Christian Warner's face remained unmarred, the tanned skin stretched tight to his blond hairline.

From time to time, rumors of the actor going under a plastic surgeon's knife hit the cover of one tabloid or another. From where she sat, she had to agree with the rumors. Even when his dimples flashed, the skin around his eyes remained impassive. Unlike Scott's. His smile claimed his entire face, including his eyes.

What was she doing? Comparing the two gorgeous men as if they were a buffet lunch. The thought was comical. However, if she had to choose, she would take the Englishman with a side salad.

No, no, no! This was not on the list. She was in Italy to find herself—not lose her head.

Isabella collected her trash and pushed away from the table. "Excuse me, gentlemen. I'm going to say goodbye. It was a pleasure meeting you, Mr. Warner. Mr. Hancock, thank you for your help."

She stood, adjusted her carry-on bag against her hip, and began to wrestle her luggage from around her chair.

"Hang on a moment, will you, Chris?" Scott stood and took hold of one of the handles. "If you can give me a few more minutes, the offer to drive you stands."

Isabella stopped. Scott's scent seemed to fold itself into her skin. What would be the harm if she accepted his offer? Hadn't she already jumped feet first, without a care for the ramifications? She had taken a leap of faith that Italy would cut through her cocoon and release her. Perhaps this was the next step.

Scott touched her arm. "Isabella, please wait. I'll only be a moment."

She looked up at him. Why not take a drink from the sweet well in front of her? An offer like this would never come along again.

Before she could speak, five women submerged the table. The *mêlée* took on a life of its own. Pens and papers flew past Isabella's face amidst a perfume fog and a maelstrom of breathless squeals.

Scott looked past the women. He motioned for Isabella to sit at a nearby table and then returned his attention to his fans. Isabella watched him grin and take a pen from a petite blonde stuffed into a pink halter top. Scott gave the woman his full attention—his smile seemingly only for her.

He was in his element, whereas she was completely out of hers.

Isabella turned and walked away.

Seven

"ASPETTA *qui per me tornare.*" The minibus tour driver repeated the phrase even though Isabella continued to shake her head.

She removed her sunglasses and increased the volume of her voice. "I don't understand what you're saying. Speak slowly." What was she doing? Did she honestly think shouting was going to break the language barrier? "Do you speak English? *Inglese.*"

The driver nodded. *"Si, aspetta qui per me tornare."*

"Do you speak *Inglese?*" Isabella shouted.

A whole lot of good the phone app was doing her now. What a piss-poor time for a dead cell. And her audience wasn't much help either. Sure, they were enjoying the show, but would one of them think to come to her rescue?

"Aspetta qui per me tornare," the driver repeated. He picked up one of her bags and loaded it behind the back seat of the van.

Isabella followed and began to climb onto the middle seat. The driver took her by the arm and pulled her back. "No. *Aspetta qui per me tornare.*" He motioned his hands to the ground. "*Aspetta qui per me tornare.*"

"I don't understand you!" she shouted. "Listen to me. I. Don't. Understand. You!"

The driver took hold of Isabella's second bag. He placed it next to the first and closed the van's sliding door. "*Aspetta qui per me tornare,*" he said as he walked to the driver's side of the van and climbed in.

"Wait! Where are you going?"

Isabella ran to the passenger door and pulled. The driver lowered the window an inch. "*Aspetta qui per me tornare.*"

"No, wait. Where are you going?" She banged on the window.

"Wait! What are you doing?"

"Can I help?" A lanky man in a flowered shirt stepped forward. "Let me talk to him." The good Samaritan spoke with the tout driver. While the Italian man gesticulated wildly, Isabella's rescuer nodded.

He returned as the van drove away. "The driver said he'll come back as soon as he collects more passengers."

"But why couldn't I go with him?"

"Something about airport rules." The man smiled, then walked back to his companions.

"Thank you," Isabella called out.

She rotated in a slow circle. Now what? She was completely bewildered about what to do next. Should she find a place to sit or stay in this exact spot? Two buses pulled in where the tout van had parked. If the buses were there when the driver returned, where would he park? How long would she have to wait? What if he didn't come back? Okay, that was foolish. Of course he'll come back. But when? She hadn't even taken his name. Or license plate number. And why was it so stinking hot? She knew July would be hot but not this hot.

Isabella looked at her watch. It was only noon. All she had to do was take a deep breath and keep her wits. She could still be at her hotel room with plenty of time to take a shower before doing a little sightseeing. While adjusting her carry-on's strap across her chest, she looked for a place to sit.

"Isabella!"

She reversed her attention and grinned at the friendly face of the short, elderly woman.

"Franny. Hi. I mean *ciao*. Where's Harry?"

"He's coming. Why are you still here?"

"Me? I… well, I had some coffee and then was going to catch a tout. I'm just waiting for the driver to come back. Why are you still here?"

"We had breakfast. It was lovely. Too bad we didn't run into you. You could have joined us."

Isabella smiled. Another invitation. First Scott and now Franny. Was Scott still here or had he left? Would she run into him at the hotel? Probably not. Her room was on the fifth floor, and he would probably be in the penthouse. Most likely with a pretty girl by his side. Why was she doing this to herself?

"We're taking the train. What hotel are you staying in? Oh, dear, Isabella, you need to get out of the sun. Do you have a hat?"

Franny's voice sounded a hundred miles away. "I'm sorry. I lost my train of thought. It's hot out here." Isabella opened her bag and removed the bottle of water Scott had purchased. Had she thanked him for the it?

"No, I don't." Isabella took a long drink before answering Franny's question about her hotel. "I'm staying at the Hassler."

"That's right near ours. We can meet tonight on the Steps. Harry and I will be there around nine. But we can finalize the plans while we're on the train. Oh, good, there's Harry." Franny waved her arms and called out. "Look who I found!"

Harry Carlson arrived, pulling two over-sized suitcases. "Hello, Isabella. You joining us on the train?"

"Hi, Harry. I mean, *ciao*. And no, I'm not. I have to wait for the tout driver."

"Harry, dear. I invited Isabella to join us tonight. I said around nine, after the children go to bed."

"Perfect. Well, we'll see you then. We'll be at the bottom of the Steps, by the fountain. Come on, Franny."

"Bye, you two. If I don't make it tonight, I hope you have a wonderful anniversary." Isabella kissed Franny's cheek.

"Goodbye, Isabella." Harry nodded at his wife. "Come on, Franny. I need a nap."

Isabella watched them enter the train station. When they were no longer in sight, she went in search of a place to sit. She claimed a seat in the shade, tucked her feet under the bench, and bent against her carry-on. She needed to get her head straight. She needed to vanquish the past so she could move on with her life. But there were too many distracting thoughts.

She unzipped her bag and withdrew a hardcover book bound in tattered, red binding. Running her index finger along the broken spine, she closed her eyes, her skin taking inventory of each crack and fissure. In one month she had come to know the book intimately—its feel and its smell.

She spread the pages and lifted the yellowed paper to her nose. Inhaling a deep draw of breath, she allowed the past thirty days to fade and give way to the first of June.

"Miss M, what do you want me to do with this box?"

"What box?" Isabella asked.

"This box." Craig held a shoe box over the hole in the ceiling. "Feels like there's something inside. Want me to open it?"

"That's okay. I'll take it." Isabella inched up the rickety ladder and stared at the box her former student held.

"Careful." Craig kept the box steady. "It's covered in dust and shit."

"Do you think there's a mouse inside?"

"Naw, I shook it. Too heavy for a mouse. Maybe a rat."

"Funny." Isabella's nose itched but she held back the sneeze. She reached and took hold of the box's sides. She kept it level to keep the thick, downy grime coating on top from spilling into her face and backed down the ladder, then placed the box in the sink and wiped the cover. The lid bore the name of McMillan's Shoes—a local store long out of business. She nudged off the cover and peered inside.

"The wiring's done." Craig jumped off the ladder. "What's in the box? Cash?"

"No. A book. And an envelope. From the look of them, they've been up there a long time. Look at this." Isabella held up the book before placing it on the counter.

"Aw, Miss M, you know I hate books. I gotta fly. If you need anything else, just call my cell."

Isabella opened the envelope. Her focus remained on the contents even though she called out to Craig. "Yes. Thank you. Your check is on the hall ta..."

None of what she saw made sense.

Isabella returned her focus to the roadway. An angry spasm rumbled against the side of the bag pressing into her abdomen. The *cornetto* was long gone—she was hungry. If she'd accepted Scott's offer, she might be at the hotel by now. Why hadn't she? She could have waited for the fans to leave. While he finished his conversation with Warner, she could have looked in the shops or read her book. What had she been afraid of? It wasn't as if there was anything romantic on the radar, so she couldn't say she had been afraid of being hurt. He was just being kind. Plus, he'd never finished what he'd started to tell her. She intrigued him. She had many qualities, but being intriguing wasn't one of them.

Maybe he enjoyed her outburst at Qualdop. Little did he know it had taken her years to muster the courage to stand up for herself. As her father had taught her, it's easier to back down. 'Why go through a pile of manure when you can go around it?' he would say. Thanks to Freddy, those early lessons had become part of her ingrained character—her knee-jerk reaction that if she asserted herself, she would be unworthy of love. 'No man wants a strong woman.' Funny how her father and Freddy had never known each other yet used the same phrase.

A cloud of exhaust blew into Isabella's face. Coughing, she wiped her eyes with the back of her hand and sighed. She had to pee.

Isabella checked the time. Three-thirty. It didn't take a rocket scientist to figure out her luggage was long gone. She was officially screwed.

Two security guards sauntered by with intimidating machine guns held close to their sides. She was hot, hungry, thirsty, and emotionally drained. Plus, she needed a shower and had to pee like a race horse. She wasn't accomplishing anything on the bench. What's the worst that could happen? They certainly wouldn't shoot her.

Mustering her resolve, Isabella stood and walked over.

"Excuse me," she called out. "Can you help me?"

"Si, signora." The young guard smiled. He couldn't have been more than twenty. The other guard was much older and wore a grizzled expression. He remained silent and eyed Isabella with a suspicious look.

"Do you speak English?" she asked the young officer.

"*Si.*"

"I gave my luggage to a minibus tout driver over two hours ago. He told me to wait here, but he hasn't returned. How can I find him?"

Grizzled-officer chuckled loudly. *"Il vostro bagaglio è andato. Stupido Americano."*

The young officer's face broke into a laugh.

She might not speak fluent Italian, but s*tupido Americano* rang loud and clear. She was in no mood for levity—especially at her own expense.

Isabella narrowed her eyes and shot the older man a nasty look. "Listen guys, this may be funny to you, but it's not to me. Can you help me or not?"

"*Signora*," the young officer said. "Your luggage, she is most likely gone. We have no way of tracking the drivers. They are, how you say, freelance. You are welcome to continue to wait."

"So, you're saying my luggage is gone?"

"*Si*, many drivers they are good. Some..." He shrugged and frowned, allowing his body language to convey his meaning.

The hunger pains in her stomach turned into cramps as a wave of nausea passed through on its way to her throat. A bitter taste of bile rose into her mouth. This couldn't be happening. Things like this only happened in movies. Added for the comedic pleasure of the audience. Look at the inane character. Haha. She's such a moron. She's going to die on a hill in Tuscany. Haha. Only this wasn't a movie. It was real, and her luggage was gone. In one second she would vomit and ruin the young officer's crisp uniform.

Isabella swallowed the mouthful of foul saliva. "There has to be a way to find him. Please, you have to help me. Perhaps I misunderstood the driver. Is there another area? Someplace else where they pick up passengers? Or someplace where I can report this?"

"*Si, signora*. I can describe how you get there to report."

Young-officer plowed into a complex set of directions that left Isabella's head spinning. Before he had a chance to repeat them, someone farther down the waiting area yelled. Both guards lifted their guns and bolted away.

"This just sucks." Isabella faced the doors leading into the airport and then turned back to the road. "Now what do I do?"

"Isabella!"

She spun around. Her pleasure at seeing him had nothing to do with him. She needed help, that was all. The fluttering in her stomach was just the excitement of the day's events, the lightheaded feeling due to dehydration and the heat, the foolish grin on her lips due to her having an emotional breakdown.

"Mr. Hancock..."

Scott furrowed his eyebrows, the three creases deepening. "Isabella, why are you still here?"

"I'm waiting."

"For?"

"My luggage."

"And, your luggage is off where? Using the loo?"

Isabella bit the corner of her lip. "No."

"Where then?"

"Gone."

"Ah, here we go again. Isabella, using a full sentence, tell me where your luggage is."

"I… I don't know."

"You don't know how to form a full sentence, or you don't know where your luggage is?"

Her voice cracked. "The latter."

Scott ran his hand through his hair. "You're not making any sense." He glanced down at Isabella's feet and looked around her legs and then back at her face. "Where is your luggage?"

"With the tout driver."

"And where is the tout driver?"

"Probably in Croatia." She added a feeble chuckle as tears began to form. "I think my luggage was stolen."

Sentences spilled out with her tears. "I spoke to the police, but they couldn't help me. They had machine guns and ran off. They said... the driver… he told me to wait. I wanted to ride with him, but he wouldn't let me. He stored my luggage in the van and sped off. I've been here since noon. I'm hungry. I'm tired. I'm thirsty. And I have to pee. He took all my clothes... my… everything except for what's in my carry-on. I'm… I'm so screwed."

"Now, now." An initialed handkerchief dangled in front of Isabella's face. "Dry your eyes. At least we know you can string together more than one or two words. I, myself, am quite thrilled."

The tears slowed as Isabella held Scott's handkerchief against her nose. She wasn't so far gone that the scent of the material didn't register. If she blew her nose in the cloth, he wouldn't want it back. Then she could keep it. His aroma was too delicious not to inhale on a daily basis.

Scott pulled her into an embrace. "Feeling better? My humor has that effect on women. Come now, we'll sort this out."

Isabella leaned against Scott, the side of her face resting on his chest. In his movies when bare-chested, he displayed the body of an older man. Instead of showing hard, sculpted muscles, he appeared strong and sturdy. The body she leaned into confirmed her impressions.

"Let me see what I can do." Scott added a gentle rub of her back and released her.

Isabella held the white cloth to her nose as he walked over to a new pair of guards. Nothing she heard made sense except for Scott's *grazie*. He signed a few autographs and then sauntered back.

"You look like you're about to drop." He took hold of Isabella's arm and led her to a nearby bench. He patted the area next to him. "Come on, luv, have a seat. I've good news and bad. Which do you want first?"

Isabella lowered herself; her brain was beginning to shut down. She needed someone to pinch her. This had to be a dream. If she woke, would she be back in New Boston, in her original bedroom? The box, the trip, Scott, all part of one convoluted dream?

"What's the bad news?" she asked, pushing her voice out of her parched throat.

Scott rested against the back of the bench. "Well, the bad news is your luggage is, most likely, in Croatia. There's no getting it back."

"You've got to be kidding me." Isabella angled to stare at him. "How on earth could there be any good news in all of this."

"The good news is I'll drive you to the hotel."

"Oh, for goodness sake, get over yourself." Isabella slammed against the bench's back and folded her arms over the top of her bag. "My luggage was just stolen, and you think riding in a car with you to the hotel will be a highlight." She turned again and glared at him. "Are you for real?"

"Hold on. There are many lassies who would enjoy riding in a car with me."

Isabella's mouth dropped open. "You are the most insufferable... egotistical... self-absorbed... I... I... I want to scream."

A devilish grin spread across Scott's face. "Yes, but you've remained seated, which means my offer is somewhat appealing."

"Ohh! You make my blood boil. I don't need a ride." She stood and tugged on her bag's strap. "There's always the train. Good day, Mr. Hancock."

Scott stood and reached for Isabella's arm. "This is getting tiresome. Please don't walk away again. You're correct. Riding with me is poor consolation when you've been robbed, which, technically, you weren't, but I would enjoy your company."

Isabella yanked her arm free. "I technically wasn't robbed? I *was* robbed—plain and simple."

Scott scratched his chin and then inserted his hands into his pockets. "Actually, you gave the man your luggage. A rather foolhardy cock-up, but—"

"A what!" Isabella's voice rose. "Cock-up! You're calling me, what, daft?"

"No, I didn't say daft and keep your voice down."

"Don't tell me to keep my voice down. I'll shout from the Vatican if I feel like it."

"I think it best that I get you out of here. And I'm not about to leave you to fend for yourself. You'll soon be joining your luggage. Now, stay here like a good girl and wait for me. My car's parked in the lot."

Scott didn't give her a chance to argue. Isabella followed his strides as he moved in the direction of the parking area, periodically stopping to autograph whatever waved in front of him.

She must look like a ninny to him. A bedraggled woman incapable of taking care of herself. Well, she would show him. Taking the train would demonstrate just how capable she was. She would like to see his face when he came back and she was gone. Actually, she *would* like to see his face.

Isabella sighed and sat back down. Her quest to find herself had just taken a major detour.

Eight

THE roar of an engine drew Isabella's eyes to the road. A sleek black convertible swung a U-turn and parked alongside the curb. Scott flashed a wide grin, revealing perfect teeth. He leapt from the car and made his way over to her. A group of women recognized him and swarmed like tittering vultures.

"Mr. Hancock," one woman fawned. "Is it true you do all your own stunts?"

Isabella watched Scott field their questions with humor, giving them his full attention. He belonged to them.

"I tried. Of course, the director fancied keeping me alive, so some required a stunt double."

"Scott, are you dating?"

"At present I'm on the market." Scott winked at the woman. She all but swooned into his arms. The rest of the group giggled and voiced more inquiries about his love life.

Scott's patience and good cheer amazed Isabella. Some celebrities shied away from the limelight while other's basked in it. He appeared to be somewhere in between.

"Thank you, ladies. I must be off." Leaving them, he walked over to Isabella and reached for her hand. "Let's go. I've a feeling the paparazzi are on the move."

Scott opened the passenger door and took hold of Isabella's bag. Isabella heard the trunk open and close. After he seated himself behind the steering wheel, Scott leaned her way and offered a grin. "Better fasten up. You're about to get a taste of driving—Italian style."

The engine purred to life. They eased out of the airport and merged onto the highway. Scott pressed the accelerator, and the car shot forward like a bullet from a gun, entering the Indy 500 car race called Italian driving—complete with roaring engines, screeching tires, and breakneck maneuvers.

Scott's speed pushed the sound barrier, yet cars still managed to zoom past. He pursued them as if in a high-speed chase from one of his movies. Added to the adrenaline-infused chaos were shouts, horns, and near misses with vehicles, motorcycles, and pedestrians.

Isabella gripped the edge of her seat. If she could remember the correct Newton's Law, she might be able to predict the direction her body would fly when they collided with a rapidly approaching rear end of a truck. But first she had to figure out how to get her stomach out of her mouth.

Scott cut the wheel to the right, avoiding the collision by a hair while Isabella squeezed her eyes shut. How on earth did she think she would be able to drive without causing a multi-car pileup?

"Buck up, Isabella," Scott chided. "Open your eyes. You're missing all the fun."

She glanced at Scott. His laughter mixed with the wind in her ears. "This is not my idea of fun."

Scott's laughter boomed. "There's nothing like driving in Italy to get the blood flowing." He increased the car's speed and they all but flew over the Tiber river. Isabella would have bet the tires actually left the surface of the bridge as they landed on the far side.

She pressed her legs together to keep her bladder from emptying. Imagine the look on Scott's face when she said, 'Thanks for the ride; you might want to get your seat cleaned.'

"Mind a little side trip?" Scott slowed the car. "I thought I'd show you some of the Borghese Gardens."

"If the side trip means getting out of the car in one piece, I'm all for it."

"You're a trooper, Isabella Martini."

Scott drove to the *Piazza del Popolo* and parked in an area marked *riservato*. He wore a shy grin and retrieved a placard from the glove box. "One of the perks that comes with fame." He placed the card on the dash and flipped a switch, bringing the car's roof over their heads. After he locked the hooks, Scott left the car and arrived at the passenger door, his hand extended. "Shall we?"

Isabella unfolded her legs and drew herself from the confines of the sports car. "That was… I will never be able to drive on these streets and come out alive."

"Nonsense. Just stay to the right and ignore the noise." Scott opened the trunk and removed Isabella's bag. "Do you need the loo?"

"Yes, please." Isabella stretched and inhaled. A new scent arrived and introduced itself. Something sweetly floral and tangy stirred on the breeze, as if the universe blessed the hot air with its own blend of perfume.

"Too bad you're not spending more time in Rome," Scott said. "It takes days to explore all Borghese's secrets. Come, I'll show you a few."

Scott swung the strap of Isabella's carry-on over his shoulder and led her along the roadway and into the gardens.

Isabella stopped at the side of the path and pointed at a rustic spot containing two narrow stone ledges. She dropped onto one of the slabs. "This is charming. If I lived in Rome, I'd come here and read."

"Rome has tens of thousands of such places. Let me walk you to the facilities, then I'll take you to an even more charming spot."

They headed up a gradual incline dotted with pine trees. Isabella craned her neck to see the smooth, molded tops. "These trees are amazing. Are these the Umbrella pines? I read about them."

"What else did you read about?"

"Not much." Isabella turned and looked at Scott. Her stomach flipped in a series of somersaults. He walked behind her, looking totally at ease in his open suit jacket and dark sunglasses. "I wanted to be surprised."

"And are you?"

"Yes. Very much," Isabella gushed. "The colors, the sounds, the aroma… I could fall in love with Rome." She wanted to twirl. Aside from looking like a fool, she might stumble and fall. Better to walk like a normal person and save the dance for the privacy of her hotel room.

"Well, you know, Rome *is* the city of love." Scott winked and handed Isabella her bag. "Don't let this out of your sight. I'll be at that kiosk getting us some water."

He started back down the hill, leaving Isabella at the door of a cream and pink stone building. She hadn't missed his comment. He'd obviously overheard her initial conversation with the Carlsons. What else had he heard? She'd told the Carlsons her name, so most likely he already knew it when they were at the café. And she'd made the comment about liking rascals. Was he a rascal? Her gut told her the answer would be a resounding yes.

Scott stood at the refreshment stand and signed autographs. Isabella walked past and settled on a wooden bench in the shade. The reality of her situation joined her. Her luggage was gone, which meant she had no clean clothes and no toiletries, except for the few items the airline had provided. The only items she was happy to lose were the loose dresses, shorts, and pants. Everything else would be missed. Her socks were gone, underwear, bras, a second pair of sneakers, and her pajamas, bathrobe, and jacket. Rome wasn't known for its inexpensive stores. Hopefully, this André, with whom she had a hair appointment in the morning, wouldn't be too expensive.

"Sorry about that." Scott stood by the bench and handed Isabella a water bottle. "Here, as a celebration of you not ending up in Croatia." He extended a string attached to a colorful, butterfly-shaped balloon.

Isabella angled her face in Scott's direction. "Thank you. Wait, *Grazie mille.*"

"*Sono particolarmente colpiti dalla sua,*" Scott replied.

"That's not fair. English, please." She laughed and stood. "Now where?"

"Down here." Scott took hold of Isabella's bag and led her along a path.

"Mr. Hancock, thank you for coming to my aid again."

"My pleasure. And please, call me Scott."

They didn't get far when a new cluster of fans stopped them. As before, Isabella moved to the side and watched Scott smile, laugh, shake hands, and pose for pictures.

He could be with anyone of his choosing. Why, then, had he chosen to spend time with her? What did he see in her that he didn't see in any of those other fans? And what did he see in her that she didn't see in herself?

They eventually arrived at *Viale del Lago*. Isabella stood mesmerized by the sight. She had seen many lakes but this… this was truly magnificent.

"Do I hear ducks?" she asked.

"Yes, on the other side. If you like, we can walk over there. However, this area tends to be more secluded. Plus, there's a stone ledge up ahead. Another one of those charming spots you seem to enjoy."

Isabella drew in a long breath. "I can't get over how delicious Rome smells. I wish I could bottle it and bring it back to New Boston with me. Tell me about that temple?" She pointed beyond the wrought-iron fencing encircling the lake. A small island housed an ancient-looking structure. Inside the stone building stood a statue of a man holding a staff coiled by a snake.

A warm hand pressed into her lower back. "Here, sit." Scott directed Isabella to a long stone slab attached to a high rock wall. "That's the *Temple of Aesculapius*. Historians believe it was built in honor of the original temple that was located on Tiber Island. Sadly, that temple is long gone. That fellow in the center there is Aesculapius with his infamous serpent."

Isabella opened her water. "There's so much to see. Perhaps I should stay in Rome and forget about Tuscany."

"I myself struggle with the same question. Shall I remain here or venture to the coast or into the hills? They all possess their own brand of beauty."

"You were born in Italy, correct?" Isabella knew little bits about him—he was fifty-five, had an Italian mother who was an opera singer, British father, spent his early years in Italy and then relocated to England after his parents divorced. Other than those sparse details, there was little else. Besides his age and acting career, he never allowed interviews to enter the personal realm of his life. She did know he'd lost a child in a car accident. And that he was divorced.

"Yes. My mum was Italian."

"Is your mother still alive?" Isabella inquired. "If I'm getting too personal, just say so. I don't mean to pry."

"Not a problem. My mum died of cancer. Started in her throat then spread. For a smart woman who lived off her voice, she was remarkably stubborn in her refusal to give up the fags." Scott chuckled at the look Isabella gave him. "Cigarettes," he explained.

"What about your father?"

Scott placed Isabella's bag on the bench and then leaned forward. He reached past his leg and picked up a twig. While twirling it around his fingers, he shook his head. "Heart attack."

"I'm sorry for your losses. Our parents are the only people who love us unconditionally, and when they die, it can be... well, it's lonely. We become orphans, in a way."

Scott sat back and stretched out his legs. "I'm inclined to agree with you on my mum's side, but regarding my father, I couldn't say. I didn't get to know him very well." He removed his sunglasses, then angled his neck and looked at Isabella. "I take it your parents are gone."

"Yes. My father suffered a massive stroke when I was fourteen. He was a good man. Tough but good. My mother never recovered from the loss. It's funny, I used to think she never pulled out of mourning because she loved him. Now I'm not so sure."

Isabella took a drink of water and then recapped the bottle. "She developed dementia while I was in college. She began wandering away from the house. I'd get calls she was missing, then found, then missing again. I moved back home after I graduated."

Isabella watched Scott for any indication that he might want her to stop reminiscing. His eyes offered encouragement to continue.

"I hired a caretaker to be with her while I was at work. Five years ago, I came home to the most surreal scene. My mother was fully aware of her surroundings." Isabella told Scott about the travel brochures and new hairstyle.

"She kept talking about a plane ticket to Italy but couldn't remember where she'd put it. She died during the night." Isabella forced a smile. "It was a good death, as deaths go. She hadn't appeared to have been in pain."

"Hm." Scott shook his head. "I've had dealings with dementia. My *nonna*. They oftentimes fabricate memories."

"No." Isabella pulled her bag onto her lap. She tied the balloon's string through the strap's metal ring before unzipping the large, outer pocket. She flashed a plane ticket in Scott's direction. "That's just it. When I was selling the house, one of my former students was in the old attic doing some wiring. He found a box. This was in it. It's dated March, nineteen sixty-four. That's eight months before I was born."

"How old was your mother when this was issued?" Scott studied the ticket, flipping it over a several times.

"She would have been thirty-two."

"And just this was in the box?"

Isabella paused. Was she revealing too much, too soon? She didn't even know this man. Yet... perhaps...

She reached into the pocket and withdrew the book. "This was in the box too."

"My word. May I?" Scott took hold of the book and caressed the red binding. "Mind if I open it?"

"Not at all. But be careful, please. It's old."

He slipped his thumb under the front cover and read the name written in the upper corner. "Christina Martini." He looked at Isabella. "Your mum?"

Isabella nodded.

Scott flipped through the pages, his fingers caressing the faded edges. He raised the book to his nose. "Perfect. Simply perfect," he murmured. "Nothing speaks like an old book." He slid the ticket against the inside of the back cover. "I gather this is where you were going when you said you thought your mother mourned your father out of love? You found this ticket and now think something else was at play?"

Isabella gave him a quick nod as her left hand sought the gold circle on her right ring finger. She methodically twisted the ring back and forth.

"Yes. Perhaps my mother's emotions centered on guilt. Maybe she was planning on leaving my father but then discovered she was pregnant. She might have stayed with him out of doing the right thing."

"Or, your mum could have suffered from remorse at not living the life she wanted. Just because a woman is pregnant doesn't mean she has to stay in a loveless marriage."

"Are you speaking from experience?"

"Well, I'm not a woman, am I?" Scott returned the book to the pocket of Isabella's bag. "I take it you're here to discover your mother's past?"

"No, but yes." Isabella jiggled her leg. A slender woman ran by, pushing a toddler in a jogging carriage. Isabella followed the runner's feet as they pounded the pavement, propelling her and the child on a direct route further into the garden. What would it be like to move forward instead of always cycling back to the past?

She cast her eyes in Scott's direction. "I don't know why I'm about to tell you this, but here goes. I cleaned out my retirement account for this trip."

Scott raised an eyebrow as he cast a skeptical look Isabella's way. "Really? Now, why would you do that? And I have to wonder why you would tell me. Are you starting to feel you can trust me?"

A faint smile appeared on Isabella's lips. "Perhaps. As for the money…" Isabella shrugged and continued. "I used the money from the sale of my childhood home to buy my new, prefabricated, adult-community house. I have a place to live and a job—but not much of a life. I hope this trip will, I don't know, give me the missing piece." She opened the water bottle and finished the remaining liquid. It trailed down the inside of her chest toward her stomach, leaving a chilling sensation in its wake.

"Ah, you're an optimist," Scott said.

Isabella frowned and gave her had a slow, methodical shake. "Not really."

"Well, from where I'm sitting, you're an optimist."

Isabella glanced at Scott. "How so?"

"For one thing, you didn't sit back in your new prefabricated house and wait for something to happen. You took control. Some might take a chance and expect the worst, but I don't believe you're in that category. And I don't believe you would have made this trip if, on some level, you didn't think it would work out. There's an optimist in you, whether you care to admit it or not."

Isabella nudged a pebble with her shoe. A series of high-pitched quacks skidded over the air. She slipped her hands under her thighs and stared at the lake and the row of boats dotting the shimmering surface.

"I appreciate the compliment," she finally said. "Unfortunately, you're off mark. I never look at the glass as half empty or half full—I just accept what's in it. I guess that makes me resigned—powerless to change the course of things. I do hope Italy might fix that part of me, along with a whole boatload of other issues. But I'm not going to bet the farm on it."

"Since you drained your funds I would say you've done more than bet the farm—

you're in the bloody race." Scott slipped his sunglasses on the bridge of his nose. The deeply tinted lenses did a thorough job at hiding his eyes. But they couldn't mask the tenderness in his voice. "You've come to the right place, lass. Italy holds amazing powers—if one believes."

She'd never put much stock in miracles. What had Franny Carlson said? 'Miracles do happen, if you believe.' Perhaps it was time to change that part of her, as well. The list kept getting longer. A month on the Mediterranean continent might not be enough time.

Nine

"I'M sorry to say, as much as I'm enjoying your company, I've a dinner date and I still need to shower," Scott announced.

His information jolted Isabella. It had been so easy to talk to him she'd forgotten he was a celebrity. Of course he had a date. He probably had three dates most nights.

"I'm sorry. I… I've taken up your time," she stammered. "Yes, let's go. I don't want the hotel to give away my room."

"If they do, you can always bunk with me." Scott reached for her bag, but Isabella turned away.

"I can carry it. Thank you," she said.

"I never said you couldn't carry it." He moved in front of her, blocking her exit. "You are a challenge, Isabella Martini." Grasping the strap with a firm hold, he removed it from her shoulder. "However, as I said earlier, I never back down from a challenge. Shall we?"

With a sweep of his hand, he motioned her along the path.

Located between a tightly-packed block of brick buildings on its right and the *Trinité dei Monti* on its left, the grandeur of the Hassler Roma lay hidden behind flesh-colored concrete. It wasn't at all what Isabella expected for a five-star hotel.

Scott seemed to read her disappointment. After he parked in front of the revolving door, he patted her hand. "Never judge a book by its cover."

An impeccably dressed doorman rushed toward Isabella's door. *"Benvenuti all'hotel Hassler Roma, signora."*

"*Grazie.*" Isabella stepped from the car.

Scott came around the front and clapped the doorman on his

shoulder. *"Buonasera, Piero. Questo è perdere Martini."*

"Buonasera, Signor Hancock. Ben tornato. Non perdere Martini ha bagagli?"

Isabella had no idea what they were saying and started to ignore the Italian streaming by when she heard the word *bagagli.* Luggage. Without any luggage, the hotel staff would think she was one of Scott's acquisitions.

"My name is Isabella Martini," she blurted. "I lost my luggage. It was stolen—at the airport. I'm a registered guest of the hotel, not of Mr. Hancock."

"Relax, Isabella. Your virtue is secure." Scott chuckled and walked past.

"Welcome, *Signora Martini.*" Piero snapped his fingers for another attendant to take care of Scott's car.

Scott returned with Isabella's carry-on. She lunged for her bag and stumbled into the cobblestone roadway. He was quick to take hold of her arm and pull her out of harm's way.

"Good show." Scott eased into a laugh. "Now the entire block knows you're a guest of the hotel. Care to share anything else?"

Isabella turned to him. "I don't want people thinking I'm here with you, that's all."

"Would that be so bad?" He cradled Isabella's elbow and maneuvered her into the hotel. "Am I such a dastardly character?"

Isabella held him with a blank stare. "No, it's just…"

Scott took hold of her shoulders and turned her forward.

Isabella took an involuntary step back and bumped against his chest.

He bent close. "As I said, never judge a book by its cover."

She was aware no sound came out of her mouth even though it opened, closed, and then reopened. The understated elegance of the lobby was magnificent.

An enormous chandelier sent facets of amber-tinted light throughout the luxurious reception area, turning the mirrored surfaces of the antique furniture and tiled walls into reflective pools. Isabella took another step back.

"Where are you going?" Scott asked.

Isabella stiffened and lifted her heel and then placed it on Scott's foot. She should hightail it out of there. "I… I need to find a clothing store."

"Nonsense." Scott held onto her arm. "You're perfectly fine the way you are. Now, smile and kindly walk forward."

Fine the way she was—not likely. If she forfeited her room, she would lose her deposit, a small price to pay for her integrity. She could perform a Google search for a Holiday Inn.

Over Scott's shoulder, Isabella caught sight of the door labeled *Rossano Ferriti, Hairdressing*. Hair appointment. Nine o'clock tomorrow morning. Under Scott's spell, she felt beautiful. Perhaps this time tomorrow she would be.

An onyx statue caught Isabella's attention. Her movements no longer belonged to her. The sculpture drew her further into the lobby. Romulus and Remus, Rome's founders, sat under a wolf's teats, reaching their hungry mouths upward.

"Tell me the story of this," she said. "This is supposed to be The Capitoline Wolf, correct?"

Scott joined her. "Yes. A facsimile. Numitor, the twin's grandfather, was about to be overthrown by his younger brother, Amulius, who would have killed the grandchildren. To save the boys' lives, Numitor ordered them placed in a basket and thrown into the Tiber River. They were eventually rescued by a female wolf who suckled them. Without her, the twins might have died. Perhaps some other kindly animal would have come along." He held Isabella's elbow and nodded to the reception desk. "Let's get you settled."

Upon reaching the desk, Scott introduced Isabella and then moved aside to speak with another clerk while she completed her registration.

When Isabella finished, she found him waiting for her by the elevator. He glanced at her room key and gave her a mischievous grin. "Five-oh-one. You've a smashing view of the Steps; plus, you're right below me."

"I… Where are you?" she asked.

"Penthouse. Care to come up for a nightcap? I've a lovely bottle of brandy."

Isabella fumbled with her key. "I… I'll probably be asleep. And you have your dinner date."

"Ah, yes, my dinner date. I'll escort you to your room first."

The doors of the elevator opened. The large mirror on the opposite wall reflected an image that froze Isabella's lungs. A wild-haired woman stared at her with bloodshot eyes.

Scott scooted Isabella into the elevator and twisted her focus from the mirror.

"Never," he insisted, "judge a book by its cover."

"I… I'm not. It's just that... I look horrid." She added a quick snicker and shrugged. "Nothing a long, hot shower and thirty hours of sleep won't fix."

"Make sure you leave time for a visit to the Steps."

Isabella gave a quick shake of her head. "I'll see them in the morning."

"Pity. At night they're unrivaled."

The ride to the fifth floor seemed to be over before it began. Isabella managed another quick glance at herself before the doors opened.

When they reached her room, Scott held out his hand for Isabella's key. He unlocked the door and swung it open. "I'll take my leave, now that I'm confident you're safely at your room. Thank you for an enjoyable day." Instead of the customary two-cheek peck, he leaned forward and placed a lingering kiss on her left cheek.

She took the opportunity to inhale his scent one last time.

Scott moved to leave. He stopped. Running his hand through his hair, he spun on his heels and faced her. "Isabella, I…"

His words hung between them. Isabella waited.

Scott lowered his brows and massaged the back of his neck. "*Ciao,* Isabella." He turned and started the walk back to the elevator.

She should say something. Anything. Tell him she was planning a makeover and she might be pretty tomorrow. Would he like to go see *Trevi* Fountain with her after she found new clothes? Would he like to take her to another garden? Would he kiss her? It'd been far too long since she'd been kissed and she suddenly found herself yearning for one—from him.

Isabella called out. "Mr. Hancock."

Scott turned, his eyebrows raised. "Yes?"

"I… the thing is…" Could she do it? Could she ask him to stay?

Her vocal chords betrayed her. "*Grazie mille,*" she said.

Scott tipped his head and resumed his departure.

Isabella entered her room. The decor should have taken her breath way with its regal elegance. She walked to the bed and placed her bag on the thick comforter. Untying the balloon, she looped the string around the bedside lamp. Next, she moved to the closet. Inside were two plush, white bathrobes. She removed one, entered the tiled bathroom, and shed her dress. She slipped into the shower and allowed the hot water stream to wash away the turmoil of the past twenty-four hours. It was time to focus on her reasons for traveling four thousand miles. It was folly to continue to think about Scott Hancock. From this point on, she would banish all thoughts of him.

Why, then, did she continue to think about him?

"I told you this trip was a bad idea. You're going to get yourself killed. Now some perverted van driver has your name and phone number." Silence followed Beth's comment. She then added, "You did write your name and phone number on all your clothes?"

Isabella placed the call on speaker. She tipped her carry-on onto the bed and began sorting her belongings. "That seemed like a childish thing to do. As if I was going to camp."

"Isabella, what if you got murdered? How would the authorities identify your body?"

"Got it. Murdered. Identification."

"You're so foolish sometimes," Beth admonished. "And naive. Hancock could have killed you."

"He wasn't going to kill me. He just drove me to the hotel. I could have taken the train, but he showed up instead. No big deal." Isabella lifted Scott's handkerchief to her nose and inhaled. If she found out the fragrance he wore, she would buy a gallon of it.

"It is a big deal. What was he still doing at the airport? I'll tell you—he was stalking you."

"He wasn't stalking me. You watch too many crime shows. He was at a meeting. I told you, Christian Warner was there. I met two gorgeous actors, and all you seem to care about is my underwear."

"You should care about your underwear a little more. What are you going to do?"

"Go shopping."

"You don't have the money to go shopping."

"I have the money," Isabella said as she leafed through her wallet. What did a haircut cost in a posh Roman salon? She should have asked when she made the appointment. Thank goodness the airline and hotel provided amenities such as toothpaste and shampoo. Maybe she'd buy some cosmetics at the salon: a new shade of lipstick and some perfume.

"Where did you get the money? You just bought a house."

"Don't worry. I won't go crazy. At least I still have my sneakers."

"And your Spanx. Thank goodness they didn't get stolen. You should come home right now."

Isabella released a loud snicker. "Seriously? Right this second?"

"Tomorrow. Get on the earliest flight and get out of that god-forsaken country. Italians are all animals."

"You sound like Qualdrip." Isabella opened her notebook and started a list. Ibuprofen would receive the number one spot.

"Who? What the hell are you talking about?" Beth spat.

"Listen, Beth. My food—"

"Forget your food. All your clothes are gone! You have nothing to wear."

"Let's talk about something else." Isabella carried the phone to her balcony. "You should see my view. I can see the Vatican from my balcony. I might go out—"

"Don't you dare! Are you crazy?"

Isabella stroked the petals of the cyclamens filling a flower box. She'd had enough berating to last a lifetime. "Beth, I'm going to hang up."

"Wait, I have news," Beth shouted.

"What news could you possibly have? I was there yesterday."

"Well, you might want to sit down for this. Are you sitting?"

"Just tell me, Beth."

"Freddy's back in New Boston," Beth announced in what sounded like a pleased voice.

"Why would I care if Freddy is in town or on the moon?"

"He hurt you. Remember how he broke your heart?"

Isabella batted one of the flower blossoms. A large insect flew out, its angry buzzing competing with the city's sounds. "Yes, Beth, I remember. May I eat my dinner now?"

"Wait. He came into the library and wanted your number."

"Tell me you didn't give it to him." Beth's uncharacteristic silence spoke volumes.

Isabella jammed herself into one of the patio's chairs. The

tightening of her stomach had nothing to do with hunger.

"You gave Freddy my phone number!" Isabella insisted. She was about to explode.

"He's changed. He got a divorce and seemed sincere. I think you should come home and talk to him."

"Sure, no problem. I'll get on a plane tonight." Isabella severed the connection. "Of all the stupid... nonsensical... foolish women." She flung her cell into the room and watched it skid across the carpet. Good thing she wasn't wearing her sneakers or she would do a jig on the contraption.

Ten

A CONTAGIOUS electricity pulsed through Rome's night air—an energy centuries old. Maybe it was time to say *arrivederci* to her former life and remain in Italy.

She pulled the cotton bathrobe tight around her waist. *"Arrivederci,"* she shouted from the balcony.

From her vantage point, she saw the colors of the night. Music, voices, and laughter mingled with intoxicating scents of spices and incense and drifted up to her nose. Inhaling deeply, she expanded her lungs until they felt ready to burst. She held onto the breath before releasing it back into the night.

It was after nine. Franny and Harry were somewhere out there. Maybe Scott too—with his date. If she were a braver woman, she would dress and venture out. But she was far from brave. In fact, she was a wimp. Otherwise, she would have asked Scott to stay.

"I need to get this guy out of my head."

She slumped against the balcony's railing and moaned. "What the hell is wrong with me? I'm in Rome, and I sound as if I'm dying of consumption. Where's my food!"

A knocked echoed through the room. Isabella patted her hair and ran by the bed for her wallet. She arrived at the door and plastered a grin on her face, then opened the door. *"Buona—"*

Scott stood in doorway. It didn't seem humanly possible for him to look even more handsome than he had that morning, but the dark navy suit seemed to be doing the trick. A loose necktie hung at an angle against a pin-striped, white shirt.

"Mr. Hancock. I… I'm not dressed." Isabella fumbled with her wallet.

The creases between Scott's eyebrows deepened. "You look dressed to me."

"I thought you had a dinner date?" Isabella pulled the robe close to her throat.

"I did. I don't fancy standing in the hall. May I come in?"

"Yes." Isabella raised her palm. "Wait! Why are you here?"

"Too late now. You already said yes." Scott entered the room. "By the way, never open your door without first checking to see who has knocked."

Rubbing his hands together, he glanced around the room, then turned her way, his eyes wide. "Come along, Isabella. Get dressed. Rome is waiting."

"Excuse me?" Isabella stood by the open door. His being there made no sense. The only thing she understood were the excited flips her stomach was suddenly doing.

"Mr. Hancock, I—"

Scott flashed his gray eyes at her. "Why do you insist on calling me Mr. Hancock? That was my father. I'm Scott. Just Scott. Now, let's get a move on. You're missing your first night in Rome."

"The thing is, M… Scott, I don't have any clothes to wear, and I can't go out in a bathrobe. Plus, I'm tired. I have a long day ahead of me tomorrow."

"Posh. Put on your frumpled frock and let's go." Scott walked over to Isabella. He swung his arm around her shoulder and drew her from the doorway. "Allow me to show you a little of this glorious city. I promise to have you home before you turn into a pumpkin. I'll even buy you a *gelato*."

His nearness became a shot of adrenaline to Isabella's heart rate and thoughts. "Mr. Han… Scott, I don't want a *gelato*. Thank you, but I want to eat my dinner and then go to sleep."

"I don't see any dinner. Do you have food stashed in your pocket?"

She could almost hear the director yelling 'action' as someone in the wings cued the room service attendant.

"*Buonasera, signora. Ah, signor* Hancock. *Buonasera.*"

"*Buonasera*, Marco." Scott instructed Marco to leave the cart and then handed him several euros. "*Grazie*."

"I could have tipped him."

"I never said you couldn't." Scott lifted the lid covering Isabella's food and frowned. "Why on earth would you order eggs on your first night in Rome?"

Isabella stormed over to the cart and snatched the cover from his hand. "You don't get to question my food choices."

"Point taken. Now get dressed." Scott removed a slice of toast from one of the plates and wandered out onto the balcony.

Isabella marched into the bathroom and began dressing in her frumpled frock. What else could she do? Scott Hancock was a force to be reckoned with.

"This way." Scott placed his palm against Isabella's lower back and pointed to the right.

His touch radiated a distracting heat, turning Isabella's leg muscles into jelly. "I thought we were going to get a *gelato* on the Steps?" she asked.

"We are."

"Then why are you taking me away from them?" Panic laced Isabella's voice as she planted her feet firmly in place. "I don't understand." She took a step to the side and then back.

Scott moved close. "No worries, luv, I'm not trying to spirit you into a dark alley."

A crooked grin flashed Isabella's way as Scott matched her steps. When she moved back, he moved forward until she felt the chill of stone against her shoulder blades. "I didn't say... then what are you doing?"

"You certainly are intriguing," Scott said. "But no worries. I'm perfectly harmless."

Isabella smirked and tried to ignore the shiver waltzing up her spine. She was starting to think like Beth. Instead of crazy thoughts about being kidnapped, she should focus on the elephant in the room. The weak knees and fluttering stomach were obvious, as was the warmth she felt whenever he came near. However, if she peeled away her physical attraction, she knew she would find a seedling of another, far more serious problem—she was dangerously close to falling for him.

"Would you care for something more substantial than *gelato*?" Scott asked.

Isabella fought the urge to run her finger along the skin between his brows. "No, thank you. A g*elato* on the Steps will be fine."

Scott scratched his chin and frowned. "Ah, yes. Well, unfortunately, you're a year too late. Rome's mayor stopped all eating and drinking on the Steps as of October last year. Something about barbarian tourists."

"What do you mean? Audrey Hepburn ate her *gelato* on the Steps." Isabella reasserted her stance.

"I assume you're referring to *Roman Holiday*." Scott grinned. "You do know that was a movie?"

"Yes." Isabella straightened her shoulders. "However, they wouldn't show it if it couldn't be done."

"True. Rome has that movie, along with others, to thank for the tons of trash littering our lovely streets. However, come back to reality, would you? Let's walk up the way. You can decide when we arrive."

Isabella allowed him to loop his hand over her arm. "You're a persistent man, Mr. Hancock."

"Smashing, we're back to my father. Fine. You're an intriguing woman, Miss Martini."

Isabella stood in place. "What do you mean by that?"

Scott chuckled. "I feel we'll need more than *gelato* when we venture into that conversation."

Caffé Ciampini sat a stone's throw from where Isabella and

Scott had stopped to speak. Scott led Isabella through the doorway and into the quaint bistro and offered a fond handshake to the older man who greeted them.

"Isabella, this is Marco. Marco, Isabella Martini."

"*Signora*, you and *Signor* Hancock do me the honor by visiting my establishment. I have a most romantic seat in the *gazebe*."

"Mr. Hancock," Isabella whispered. "I'm not dressed for a restaurant. Please, can we just get our ice cream and leave?"

Scott reached for her hand and placed it on his forearm. He covered it with his own and bent close. "Relax. And it's called *gelato*."

Isabella rolled her eyes. "Easy for you to say. You're in a suit."

"It doesn't matter what I'm wearing. It'll always be called *gelato*," Scott said.

"No, not the ice... *gelato*. The relax part. I'm in a frumpled frock, as you called it."

"No one will look at your frock if you smile. That's the first thing that got my attention." Scott offered a corner of his grin and squeezed her hand. "However, if you feel strongly about this, we'll leave."

Isabella chewed her lip. She *was* hungry, and the prospect of sitting in a romantic setting with him was too alluring to pass up. "I am rather hungry. Perhaps a bite before my ice cream."

"*Gelato*, and smashing. This way." Scott directed Isabella onto the gazebo where they found Marco engaged in conversation with two elderly patrons.

"Isabella!" Franny Carlson leapt from her chair. "Oh, how wonderful. Marco, may we have two more chairs?"

"Of course, *Signora* Carlson."

Before Isabella could respond, she was pinned by the pint-sized Hercules. "Harry, look who it is."

"Franny, let the woman go so she can sit." Harry stood and

kissed Isabella's cheek. "Good to see you again."

"Hi, Franny. I mean *ciao. Ciao,* Harry," Isabella called over Franny's head.

"Who might you be?" Franny Carlson arched her neck. "Oh, my." The older woman's eyes popped open as she looked from Scott to Isabella and then back to Scott. "You're the handsome young man from the plane."

"Franny, let them sit. I'm sure you'll get all the details." Harry shook Scott's hand and introduced himself. "This is my wife, Franny, the busybody."

Scott bent and took hold of Franny's hand. He kissed the back and smiled. "A pleasure. I'm Scott Hancock."

"Franny, Scott is—"

Scott caught Isabella's eye and gave a slight shake of his head. "Here you go, luv, have a seat." He pulled out the chair Marco delivered, then quickly bent over and whispered, "Let's keep what I do between us."

Isabella nodded. "As I was about to say, this is so exciting to run into the two of you. Did you have your *gelato*?"

"Oh, we tried. But a nice policeman reminded us we couldn't eat our cones on the Steps, so we walked along a lovely road and ended up here. What about you?"

"Well, I was... Scott showed... I had ordered..." How should she explain the situation?

Isabella noticed the sly grin Franny wore. For an eighty-two-year-old, there were no flies on her.

"So, what do you do, Scott?" Harry asked.

"I'm in travel," Scott responded. "Isabella, have you told Franny and Harry about your encounter with the tout driver?"

Isabella smiled at Scott's ability to deflect questions back to the Carlsons. They never seemed to catch on that they knew less about him than when he sat down. Would he be as evasive if she were to question him about his life? While they sat in the Borghese Gardens, he'd answered her inquiries, hadn't he? Although she had done most of the talking. Just as the Carlsons were doing now.

"You need clothes." Sincere concern laced Franny Carlson's voice. She looked at Harry. "Do you think Margaret has some spare things?"

"Franny, don't worry," Isabella said. "I'll figure something out."

"Actually," Scott interjected. "I'll be taking Isabella about in the morning."

"Oh, how lovely." Franny added a faint giggle.

Isabella looked at Scott. "I don't—"

"I wanted to surprise you." Scott's steel-gray eyes pinned her.

The furnace under Isabella's skin kicked on. "But—"

"Where will you go?" Franny asked.

Isabella shook her head and looked at her. "Franny, we won't—"

"I've a few mates who own several shops," Scott said. "I happened to overhear you two met in Rome. I'd love to hear the story firsthand."

Franny and Harry retold their love story while Isabella thought over the day. At no point had she and Scott discussed clothes shopping. He was making an assumption. What else did he assume—the sleeping arrangements?

Her thoughts were cycling too fast. Now she was the one making assumptions. Scott hadn't hinted at kissing her, let alone sleeping with her. Yet the thought was delicious to ponder. Would she go to bed with him? What about her heart?

Scott and Harry began an animated conversation involving the salt and pepper containers as props.

Isabella watched Scott break a bread stick into small pieces and then place them in a circle around the salt grinder. His long fingers held her attention. Screw her heart—she'd survive. Plus, she wouldn't need to fantasize about any more movie sex scenes; she'd have her own.

"When do you leave for Tuscany?" Franny asked.

Isabella tugged her attention from Scott's hands. "I'm taking the train back to the airport tomorrow. I'll pick up my rental and drive up the coast, then into *Camaiore*. Hopefully, I'll get there by late afternoon."

"That won't leave us much time for shopping." Scott entered Isabella's and Franny's conversation. "I'd be happy to secure you a room for another evening."

"Oh, that would be lovely. We could visit the Colosseum together," Franny said. "You'd get to meet Harry's family."

"Now, Franny. Let the them have their time alone." Harry hugged his wife's shoulder. "After all, Rome *is* the city of love," he added before kissing her cheek.

The two couples eventually moved outside. Harry tried to hand Scott money for the dinner bill. Scott wrapped his jacket around Isabella. Before she could thank him, he moved to the side to talk with Harry. Franny took Isabella by the hand and drew her near the stone wall.

"Isabella, I thought you didn't know Scott. How on earth did you ended up dating him?"

"I'm not dating Scott. He helped me this morning…" Had it only been this morning? So much had happened, she'd have bet three days had passed.

"You can protest all you want, but these old eyes see more than you think. I do so enjoy young love."

Isabella laughed. "I'm far from young, and there is absolutely *nothing* going on between Scott and myself. He's…" Isabella's teeth tugged at the corner of her lip. He's what? Unlike any man she'd ever met?

"He just keeps appearing." Isabella angled her head as she drew the edges of Scott's jacket together.

Franny face beamed. "Oh, wonderful. Let's exchange numbers. Maybe you'll be coming back to Italy to celebrate your own wedding anniversary. Do you use email?"

Isabella tapped her phone and laughed. "You're a hoot and yes, I use email."

After they exchanged contact information, Isabella mentioned her upcoming hair appointment the following morning. While they discussed possible styles, Scott and Harry joined them.

"It was an absolute pleasure." Scott reached for Franny's hand. "I hope we meet again."

"Oh, yes. I do too," Franny exhaled.

After a quick shake of Harry's hand, Scott faced Isabella. "Shall I get our cones?"

Isabella watched Harry and Franny link hands and then start down the brightly lit sidewalk. She hoped she saw them again. The thought pleased her. Perhaps her emotional prison was unlocking. Maybe she *should* stay another night.

"I'm sorry." Isabella turned her head and looked over her shoulder at Scott.

"Our *gelato*. If we walk down this avenue, we'll come at the Steps from the base. What flavor would you like? I recommend the chocolate."

"Yes, fine. Chocolate. Thank you. I mean, *grazie*."

"Il piacere è tutto mio," Scott replied.

"No fair," Isabella chuckled. "You can't keep doing that. Pick a language. And you have to use it for the remainder of the night."

"Scelgo italiano. E 'il linguaggio dell'amore, lo sai." Scott winked and bowed. *"Attendere qui."*

The last words Isabella knew. The mini tout driver had repeated them enough times to brand her brain cells. *Wait here*. Only the driver hadn't winked or bowed. And she hadn't been wearing his jacket.

Eleven

"HERE you go. One chocolate *gelato.*" Scott handed Isabella a cone. The thick confection swirled around a golden waffled cookie.

"The biscuit is a *pizzelle,*" Scott said. "Shall we walk?"

They meandered down the steep, narrow sidewalk of *Via di S. Sebastianello* and came to a pedestrian path and followed it to *Piazza di Spagna.*

"How's your *gelato*?" Scott asked.

"It's wonderful." Isabella took a mouthful of chocolate. Her taste buds danced as coffee, cinnamon, and dark cocoa slid along her tongue. "How do you say wonderful in Italian?"

"*Meraviglioso.*" Scott said.

"*Meraviglioso,*" Isabella repeated. "It's absolutely *meraviglioso.*"

"*È assolutamente meraviglioso.*"

"Okay, no more Italian. Speak the King's English, please."

Scott bowed with a flourish. "Right-o, mum. As you wish."

Isabella stopped walking. "What did you mean when you said I intrigued you?"

Scott spun to face her. "Right. I keep getting sidetracked."

"Yes. I've noticed you're a good at evasion. This time I'm not letting you off the hook."

"Fair enough. Come with me." Scott slipped his hand over Isabella's and led her to a grassy area with benches. Scott handed his cone to her, removed a fresh handkerchief and placed it on the bench. He patted the cloth-covered stone. "Sit. Now, what was the question?"

"Nope, not going to work this time. You know the question."

"Right. I must say, you are much more at ease tonight, Miss

Martini. Tell me, is it my magic or Rome's?"

"Mostly Rome's." Although she had to confess he played a large part in the feelings coursing through her veins at the present time. "I never thought I'd say this, but I love Rome. I love the fierce energy. If I had known I would feel like this, I wouldn't have reserved the villa in *Camaiore*. I'd stay here for the month."

Scott took his time responding. His eyes explored Isabella's face. "Italy is like a lover. To truly know her, one should discover all of her."

His sensuous description seemed to melt some of her ice cream. "Um, I… since I'm a woman, perhaps Italy should be a man."

Scott leaned her direction and raised an eyebrow. "Only if you plan on discovering all he has to offer."

"You're playing with me, Mr. Hancock, and you're still evading my question."

"I don't play with people, Miss Martini." Scott licked the edge of his cone. "What do you do in New Boston, New Hampshire?"

"I'm the head librarian at a local school. And answer my question."

"What do you do for fun in your spare time?"

"Well, I go to the movies, I read, I… no, no, no. Stop. You want to know what I think?"

"Yes, what do you think?" Scott said.

"I don't think you were intrigued by me. I've been making a fool of myself about this, and you're enjoying the show."

"Guilty as charged. But not the part about you intriguing me. You did. And you still do. What does your better half do for fun while you're reading?"

"If you're asking if I'm in a relationship, I'm not. What's your game?"

"I don't play games. Perhaps I'm flirting. Not doing a bang-up job from what I can see, but I am giving it the old college try."

"Save it, Mr. Hancock. And while you're at it, you can add this clothes-shopping excursion we're supposed to be going on."

Scott laughed and shook his head. "You are a cheeky crumpet."

Isabella gripped her cone and felt it crack. "I'm not cheeky, and I'm not a crumpet, which to my knowledge is a piece of pastry. I'm very happy, Mr. Hancock. Very happy. You don't know anything about me. Just because I'm traveling alone doesn't mean I'm lonely. I love my life. It's full and rich." Isabella's voice rose. "And I don't need a man just because he's handsome and charming."

"What's got your panties in a bunch?"

"I just don't like what you implied, that's all."

"Miss Martini, I didn't imply anything."

"Yes, you did. Men like you always think a woman is ready to faint as soon as you flash your dashing smile. But that won't work on me."

"You think my smile is dashing?" Scott asked.

Isabella prayed she wouldn't lose her train of thought as she stared at him. "I keep asking you questions, and you keep giving me vague answers. You had dinner tonight with a beautiful woman who was most likely weak at the knees at the thought of going to bed with you, but you chose instead to spend the end of the evening with me." The grin he wore almost derailed her. "Did she turn you down? Is that why you ended up at my door? Am I your consolation prize?"

"Now who's making assumptions? And how did you know my dinner date was a ravishing woman willing to romp with me? Are you stalking me, Miss Martini?"

"I know men like you."

"Ah, well, as someone once said to me, you don't really know anything about me, now, do you? Allow me put the matter straight," Scott added. "I had dinner with an associate. I'm confident I could get him into bed since I know for a fact he does prefer men. However, I've chosen to not give up on the female gender quite yet. Thus far,

I'm batting zero, as you Americans like to say, but never say die. As to why I'm with you? I've a theory that under your Medusa persona there's a woman I might enjoy getting to know. And I'm hoping you might start feeling the same way. "

Isabella remained silent and focused on the dark liquid seeping between her fingers.

"Which brings us back to my being intrigued. Shall I begin?"

A horn beeped, people laughed, music played, and Isabella sat quietly biting her lower lip.

"I'll take your silence as a green light," Scott said. "Allow me to get the clothes topic out of the way. What sort of man would I be if I left you to fend for yourself in one of the most expensive cities in the world?"

"I—"

"Nope, this is my turn. I have no doubt you'll get one, but for now, you must enjoy your *gelato* and stay silent. As I mentioned at dinner, I know several shop owners and would be happy to assist you. I had every intention of asking, but the Carlson's called my hand."

"But—"

"Still my turn. Your appearance can't disguise your laugh."

"Great, now—"

Scott patted Isabella's knee. "I'm not done. When I arrived on the plane, you caught my eye. I immediately wondered what sort of woman hides from life yet flies to a foreign country—alone. I became intrigued, which continues to grow with each passing moment."

"How do you know I hide from life? Fuck." Isabella sprang from the bench.

"I beg pardon." Scott watched with an amused expression.

Isabella sprang from the bench. "I said, fuck!"

Scott grinned. "Are you asking me for a shag?"

"I'm dripping all over the place."

"I have that effect on women."

"Please get your mind out of the gutter. My *cone* is dripping. I'm making a mess." A large brown stain soaked into the linen creases of Isabella's dress. "My shift is ruined."

"More's the pity." Scott offered his handkerchief. "This is the only one I have. Will it do?"

"Thank you." Isabella traded her broken cone for the initialed cloth and began wiping at the brown splotch. Franny Carlson would have a field day if she were here.

Scott carried the cones to a bin and proceeded to a refreshment cart. He returned and reached for his handkerchief. After he wiped his hands, he held a half-empty bottle of water steady. "Hold out your hands." He poured the remainder of the water over Isabella's hands and then handed her the damp cloth.

"There isn't much we can do to save your frock. It would be best to give it a proper burial."

Isabella glared. "This dress wasn't cheap."

"Cheap or not, it's not flattering. You asked me how I knew you hid from life." Scott inclined his head at Isabella's dress. "Your appearance completed the puzzle."

"Let me get this straight." Isabella jutted her chin. "You think I'm intriguing but disapprove of my style of clothes; and you think I'm hiding behind a Medusa-like persona. Did I miss anything?"

"I didn't say I disapprove of your style of clothes. And you missed your sturdy spine and determined spirit. You're fearful yet curious, lost yet have an amazing inner navigation system. As I said, you intrigued me. After getting to know you, you beckon me."

Twelve

ISABELLA took a wide step away. "May we go see the Spanish Steps now?" She turned and sprinted across the street.

Scott reached her side and matched her quick strides. "Slow down, or you'll miss the magic."

Isabella stopped but remained facing forward, her breathing coming in deep, rapid bursts. "What magic?"

"You'll see." Scott hooked his arm around her waist. "When I tell you to close your eyes, don't ask why. Just do it like a good girl."

Before they reached the end of the block, Scott held Isabella still. "Close your eyes."

"Why—"

"Just bloody do it."

"Fine," Isabella huffed. "They're closed."

"Trust me." Scott stood behind her. Under his guidance, Isabella walked straight and then turned to the left. He held her shoulders and said, "Open your eyes."

With her breath stuck somewhere between her lungs and mouth, Isabella's eyes focused on the magnificent sight towering above her. Brilliant light encased the entire area, turning the double-spired *Trinita dei Monti* into a beacon shining down onto the immense crowd. Under the thousands of feet lay the Steps, pulsing with life. Dozens of spotlights lit the scene aflame.

"What's the Italian word for magic?" Isabella asked.

"*Magia*." Scott said.

"*Magia*," Isabella murmured. "You were right. This is *magia*."

"*Questo è magia*," Scott whispered in her ear.

"*Questo è magia*," Isabella repeated.

"She becomes more magical each time I return home."

They walked to the fountain at the base of the Steps and sat on the concrete edging.

"What's the significance of the boat?" Isabella angled and pointed to a statue of a sinking boat behind them.

Scott rested against the iron railing. "*Fontana della Barcaccia* translates into *Fountain of the Old Boat.* Legend has it a boat landed here during one of Tiber's overflows."

"All the way over here from the Tiber?" Isabella cast a skeptical glance at Scott. "Seems pretty implausible."

He shrugged. "Most of our legends are. For example, do you know the legend about the Steps?"

The temperature of the night air had dropped, and Isabella snuggled deeper into Scott's jacket. "No. Enlighten me."

"If you stand at the base of the Steps and make a wish, you'll find your true love."

"Get out. You're kidding. Where did that legend come from?"

"Your movie, *Roman Holiday.* It was on the Steps where Audrey Hepburn's character and Cary Grant's character first noticed each other."

"I don't believe it," Isabella scoffed. "If your movie career tanks, you should start a tour company."

"I have other plans, and it doesn't involve crowds. I'm hoping to locate one special woman to join me in my isolation. I can only hope I'll be as fortunate as Harry Carlson."

"How so?" Isabella angled her neck to look up at Scott. It startled her to find he had been focused on her instead of the water.

Scott cleared his throat. "Mayhaps I'll find her on these Steps. She'll be wearing a large chocolate *gelato* stain on her frock."

Isabella felt the scrutiny of Scott's eyes on her. It would be far too easy to get swept along by his tsunamic force. What then?

"It's too late," Isabella finally said as she looked away.

"I beg pardon?" Scott brushed a curl from Isabella's forehead.

"I... I meant to say it's late."

"Perhaps it is," Scott murmured as he stood and reached for her hand. "And perhaps it 'tisn't."

They started the steep ascent. By the time they reached the *Piazza di Spagna*, a furnace of pain blazed within Isabella's legs, and her heart threatened to explode out of her rib cage. Scott, however, looked as if he had just finished a pleasant stroll along the Tiber.

"Do you want to rest or keep climbing?" he asked.

"Rest, please. And sit." Isabella claimed a spot on the steps and leaned against the side of the stone wall.

Scott sat to her right. "May I?" He slipped his hand under hers and ran his thumb along the surface of the ring.

Isabella focused on the feel of her hand in his. It was warm in there and safe. Why would she trust him with her secrets but not herself?

"We've all been hurt. A person doesn't get out of this life without suffering some form of damage," he said.

"I'm aware of that. Pain and suffering are inevitable."

"But misery is optional. Why, then, do you shroud yourself with misery?"

Isabella moved to stand, but Scott reached out and returned her to sitting.

"Look at me, would you?"

Isabella gave him an icy glare.

"I'll most likely regret this," Scott said, "but here goes. You're running. That's plain to see. From what, I can only imagine. Tell me, what brought you to Italy? You said it wasn't your mother's mystery. Does it have something to do with this ring you wear? It's a wedding ring, but you wear it on your right hand."

She pulled her hand, but his hold remained steady. Her eyes narrowed into slits, made all the more caustic by her voice. "You know nothing about this ring or me."

"I didn't say I did. Although I am perceptive."

"Hm, well do you perceive that I'd like my hand back now?" Isabella snapped.

Scott released his hold and quickly ran his hand through his hair. "Bugger all, Isabella. I'm not a bloody fool. Was your heart shattered so completely that you can't find a way around it?"

"You wouldn't understand." Isabella scraped at the stain on her dress.

Scott handed her the damp handkerchief. "Try me."

Isabella remained quiet. Scott seemed content to allow her time to respond. The thoughts were entangled with her emotions. If she shared too much, he might think she was off kilter. Not enough, and he would give her the same blank expression Beth seemed to favor.

Eventually, Isabella said, "I've been the primary spectator to my life—never a participant. That's why I'm here."

"Why Italy? Was it the ticket? The book?"

"Yes and no." She sighed. "Both. I read the book and in the first chapter… the words." She dug her fingers into her hair, only to have Scott retrieve them and weave his fingers with hers.

"I'm listening."

"There was this line about the character's clothes—how they made her practically invisible. The author went on to describe the character's non-arresting face, the reluctant way she spoke…how she seemed to disappear—fade into the background."

Isabella knew the tears were there. She could feel the burning, yet she refused to grant them freedom. Instead, she continued. "You see, as I read the story, I felt I was waking from a long slumber. I'd spent a lifetime pretending to be happy while trying to forget I wasn't. What's happiness anyway? It's a fleeting emotion. But when it's gone and there's no way to find it, the loss can be suffocating." She shifted on the cold stone. "I bet you're sorry you asked."

Scott cupped her chin and turned her head. "I'm not sorry. Let me help you."

Isabella gritted her teeth. "Why? Look at yourself, then look at me. You think I'm a fool, but I know your game." Isabella pulled away from his touch.

"My game again. I told you before, I don't—"

"Get off it. You use people to get what you want." Men like Scott Hancock took what they wanted and then moved on, without regard for the damage left in their wake. It had nothing to do with his being a movie star. Freddy had taught her that. Even a man from rural New Hampshire was capable of vainglorious behavior.

Scott's mouth set in a firm line. The muscles of his jaw thickened. He remained staring at Isabella. "Tell me something, Isabella. Why is it you have no problem insulting me at will? Do you think just because I take on a character's persona, I don't have feelings?"

Isabella remained silent and clenched her teeth.

"Okay," Scott said. "I'll play along. What is it you think I want?"

The sounds of laughter spilled up the Steps. Isabella chewed her lip and faced forward.

"Cat got your tongue?"

Isabella stood. "I'm going back to the hotel now." She handed Scott his jacket and added, "Thank you for dinner and ice cream."

Scott added a laugh and straightened. "*Gelato.*"

"What-the-fuck-ever," she spat. "Good night, Mr. Hancock."

"Bloody hell. You are mad as a bag of ferrets. Why do you feel you can say whatever you want without regard for the damage you leave in your wake? And why is it a bloke can't be nice to you without having some ulterior motive?"

Isabella watched Scott's expression. A darkness settled over the lips no longer smiling. She could feel the same darkness embracing her. He wasn't allowed to use her words. Other people caused damage, not her. She was the one left dealing with their mess and the pain. She was the one left alone. She was the one who had been suffering. She… She had been so blind. Freddy hadn't left her; she had driven him away.

"It's high time I ask you what you've been tossing at me. What's your game, Isabella?"

"You've been wasting your time, Mr. Hancock." Isabella cringed as the words gained voice. "I'm not going to bed with you."

Scott folded his arms and released a caustic laugh. "When did I ever say I wanted to bed you?"

Isabella clutched the stone railing. The Steps, and the people on them, faded away as she felt her entire body become rigid. The shock of his comment spread out in waves, circling her throat and then her lungs. She had to get away from him. And fast.

Isabella turned and bolted up the last few steps, then ran for the street.

The sound of Scott's shoes hitting the concrete pushed her forward. Without looking, she entered the roadway. The screech of tires froze her. Bracing herself for the impending impact, she felt her feet leave the cobblestones.

Scott's hands held her as he set her down in front of the hotel. "Isabella, look at me. Are you okay?"

"Will you *please* stop rescuing me?" she demanded.

Isabella pulled herself free and raced into the hotel's lobby. She would be damned if she cried in front of him.

Scott followed. He reached out and regained hold of her arm. Moving her to a corner of the lobby, he faced her. "Give it up, would you? You're behaving like a child." His eyes took on the hue of an impending storm. "What I said, it was—"

Isabella's eyes shot wet daggers. "I heard what you said. Let me go."

"Keep your voice down. We don't need the bloody hotel to know our business."

"You don't get it, do you, Hancock? *We* don't have any bloody business. Now, let go of me."

"Not until you calm down and hear me out."

Isabella gnashed her teeth together and wrenched her arms out of Scott's grip. "I heard you. I heard every bloody word you said. So, do us both a favor and piss off."

"Isabella—"

"Goodnight, Mr. Hancock. And goodbye."

Choosing to avoid the elevator, Isabella ran to the fifth floor, hoping to outrun the confusion and embarrassment dogging her.

Thirteen

WHILE the lifeblood of Rome pulsed outside the hotel, Isabella's mind entered a dream that tossed her about as if she were a rag doll. While her conscious mind remained asleep, her subconscious woke to the aroma of bacon and coffee. Upon opening her eyes, she recognized her room. The sounds of her mother in the kitchen carried through the bedroom door. She bolted from the bed and ran along the hallway.

"Ma? What's going on? What are you doing?"

"Good morning to you too. I'm making breakfast like I do every morning. How do you want your eggs?"

Christina Martini stretched up on her toes. Icy fingers gripped Isabella's chin. "You're warm, Isabella. Are you feeling okay?"

"You know me?"

"Silly. Of course I know you. Here, have some coffee."

Her mother's fingers were cold. This had to be a dream. She was in Italy. Yet she could smell bacon frying in the pan. The coffee mug felt hot.

"Freddy's in the living room," Isabella's mother said. "He needs to talk to you. But I want you to wait a minute. I have to tell you something before I leave."

"Leave? Wait. Leave for where? What's going on? How do you know me?"

"I know you because I'm your mother." Isabella's mother slipped into a coat. She centered her eyes on her daughter. "Do you remember the princess game we used to play?"

"You're not making sense. Wait. Where are you going?" Isabella shook. Hot coffee spilled over her fingers. It instantly cooled to the temperature of ice water. "What the fuck is going on?"

"Isabella, language," her mother scolded. "I told you I have to leave. Now, listen. You found the box. Good for you. I completely forgot I put it up there. If your father had known about the ticket, he would have torn it up. I was planning on telling him and then discovered I was pregnant. This isn't what I wanted to tell you. Remember when we would play our princess game, and we'd choose new names? What was the name I always chose? Do you remember?"

"I was, what, six when we played that?" Isabella squeezed her eyes shut. This was it. She was losing her mind and would spend the rest of her life in an Italian asylum.

"You must remember, Isabella. Try. May I have my ring before I go?"

"Your ring?" Isabella raised her hand. The ring evaporated. When she looked at her mother's hand, it appeared. "What the fuck!"

"Isabella, language." A pair of frigid lips grazed Isabella's cheek. "I love you. I always will." Her mother vanished.

"Now what?" Isabella turned off the burner under the frying pan. She finished the make-believe coffee while looking around the kitchen. It was back to the way it had been before she'd packed up her life. Even the ugly table was there. And the torn chair.

And Freddy.

Isabella placed the mug in the sink. She took a piece of bacon from the pan and walked into the living room.

"Hello Freddy."

"Izzy, I'm glad you came." Freddy rose and wiped his hands on his pants. His blond hair framed the slender face. "Do you have time to talk?"

"Make it quick. I have a hairdresser's appointment, and I still need to return to Italy."

"Yeah, Beth told me. I never would have expected you to take a trip like that on your own. I'm proud of you."

"Save it. What do you want?"

Freddy lowered himself back onto the couch. "Aren't you going to sit down?"

Isabella remained standing and chewed the strip of bacon. Salty. Warm. Slightly crispy. She wasn't losing her mind—she had lost it.

"I'm back in town now and wondered if we could see each other."

"No. Next question."

"Come on, Izzy. You can't still be angry. That was over fifteen years ago. You need to move on."

Isabella balled her hands into fists, her right hand crushing the remaining bacon. "Don't tell me what I need to do or not do."

"You always could carry a grudge. Remember the time I stayed away for three weeks? It took me a month to get you to forgive me."

Isabella turned to leave. "If you're hoping to travel down memory lane, you can do it without me."

"I believe you have something to tell me?" Freddy crossed his legs and spread his arms across the back of the couch. He flashed a Cheshire-cat grin.

"I have nothing to tell you."

"I think you do. When you were talking to Scott, you realized you might have been to blame for some of our problems."

"Freddy, you treated me like shit—insulted me, belittled me, embarrassed me in public. You basically bullied me, and you want *me* to apologize?"

"Hey, they were your thoughts, not mine. You came to a revelation tonight, and now you're reneging." He supported his left elbow and tapped his chin with his index finger. "Let's see. What was it you realized?"

He rose and took a quick step in Isabella's direction. "I may have bullied you, but you weren't innocent. Say it."

"No."

"Say it."

"Fine," Isabella screamed. "I'm sorry. I'm fucking sorry. I was as destructive as you. Okay? I hurt people… I acted like I was the only fucking person who had feelings."

Isabella clawed at her hair. A piece of bacon fell from the tangles onto the worn carpet. She stepped on it—pushing it deeper into the tan pile. She had to say it. She would never be free if she didn't. Is this why Scott had come into her life? So she would learn the hard truth about herself?

She raised her face and whispered, "I bullied you. I said whatever I wanted. I drove you away, and I've been blaming you since you walked out the door. Are you happy?"

"The question is: are you?"

Just as her mother had done, Freddy disappeared.

A butterfly-shaped balloon peeked around the corner of the doorway. Isabella followed it out onto the back porch and watched it lift through the barren trees. A hint of cashmere passed on the air.

That was Scott's fragrance. Cashmere. He was in the house. She needed to apologize to him.

Isabella walked off the deck and searched for him.

"Hello." Isabella winced at the sound of her voice. With each pump of her heart, her brain cells recoiled.

A chipper female voice spoke through the intruding handset. *"Buongiorno. Questo è ti svegli chiamata."*

"Excuse me?" Isabella whimpered. Somebody had to have stomped on her head during the night.

"*Signora*, this is your wake-up call."

"*Grazie*," Isabella mumbled. She struggled to replace the receiver on its cradle and then draped her arm over her eyes. She needed coffee. And a dozen ibuprofen. "Why did I place a wake-up call for six o'clock?"

The dream from last night cycled by as thoughts of Scott waited for their cue. She pushed him further into the wings and focused on the two main attendees. She was smart enough to know her subconscious had put the words into her mother's and Freddy's illusory mouths.

She reached into her hair, expecting to find the remains of the bacon. Holding up her hand, she rotated her wrist. The gold band shone in the early morning light streaming through the window. Remember, her mother had said. Remember what? The game? That had been so long ago—in a different part of her life.

An offending horn blared in the street outside the hotel. More horns joined in as shouts ensued.

Isabella tossed off the comforter and sat on the edge of the bed. Blue-and-purple-tinted mylar sparkled against the checkered carpet.

"You poor thing. Tuckered out from your nocturnal flight?" Isabella untied the balloon and walked out on the balcony. She looped the string around the window box's clip and watched as the balloon dropped behind a wrought-iron chair. "Afraid to fly?" she whispered.

Taking responsibility for her emotional inertia was like lancing a festering wound. Healing wouldn't come otherwise.

Does a caterpillar feel pain? she wondered. Does it scream within its self-imposed prison as it transforms? Does it wonder if it had done something different that it might have gone on being a caterpillar? Or does it embrace the change—accepting that suffering is part of the process?

Isabella swept her eyes from the balloon to Vatican City. The gilt ball at the top of St. Peter's *basilica* reflected the morning sun like a fiery phoenix. Soon, she would spread her own wings.

Fourteen

THE decor of Rossano Ferretti was a far cry from The Cutting Edge in New Boston. Isabella stood a little straighter. She reflexively smoothed her hair, then her dress, and chastised herself for not wearing lipstick. She passed an expansive ceramic pot of fuchsia-tinted orchids and took tentative steps toward a man standing behind a black, lacquered reception desk. Perfectly sculpted cheekbones, a narrow nose, pastel lips, and luxurious black lashes graced a face typically reserved for an angel. Da Vinci himself couldn't have improved the young man's features.

He glided from around the desk and up to her. "*Buongiorno, signora. Sono Fernando, come posso aiutarvi?*" he said.

"*Buongiorno, Fernando.*" The phrase she had practiced scampered away, leaving her tongue flagging for something to say. "Um, English?"

"Si, *signora*. I speak the English."

"I have an appointment...at nine...for a haircut," Isabella stammered. "With André."

Antonio led Isabella to a black leather chair. "Please, you make yourself comfortable. André will be with you *un minuto*."

Isabella marveled at the bright Roman sunlight spilling through an arched window offering a commanding view of the same gilt ball she had admired earlier. With the view that surrounded them, how anyone in Rome accomplished anything was beyond her. She would spend the bulk of her time lost in wonder.

Antonio reappeared with a *cappuccino* and a plate of *biscotti*, then scurried away.

A short while later, he returned, accompanied by a thin woman who would rival Scott in height even if she wasn't wearing two-inch heels. A ponytail the color of corn silk swung as she walked, the satin ends draping over her slender shoulder with each turn of her head.

Red lips parted into a wide smile. "*Buongiorno.*" The woman settled in a chair opposite Isabella and reached for a *biscotti*. "What are we doing for you today?"

Isabella eyed her suspiciously. Why did she have to explain herself to the person who would be washing her hair? Maybe André was too busy to talk to his clientele. If that was the case, then she would find another stylist.

"I'll wait for André. Thank you."

An uncontrollable fit of laughter overtook the woman. "Hon, I'm André."

Isabella opened her eyes in shock. "I'm sorry. André must be short for Andrea."

"Nope, you've got it right. I'm André, not Andrea. My father had a thing for André the Giant and was hoping for a boy." André finished her cookie and wiped the crumbs off her black capris. "My mother said

I arrived, the look on his face was priceless."

Isabella laughed along. "I'll bet. At least you have the height."

"Not quite. But close. Where are you from?"

"New Hampshire. You sound American." Isabella watched André. She liked the tall woman—her confidence, poise, bright eyes, and expressive laugh.

"Born and bred. Manhattan. How long are you staying in Italy?"

"A month. I'm leaving Rome today to drive to Tuscany."

"Where in Tuscany?"

"*Camaiore*."

"Hey, I have in-laws in that region. *Viareggio*. Are you staying with friends?"

"Nope, just me. I'm renting a villa."

"Gutsy." As she talked, André stood, walked behind Isabella, and started fingering the frizzled curls. "Home perm?"

Isabella reached up and touched the wires. "No." She chuckled. "It cost me one hundred and twenty dollars, but the stylist colored my hair first."

"Hm, I can think of better ways to spend a hundred and twenty bucks." André finished her assessment and was back in the chair. "What do you have in mind?"

"I'm pretty much in your hands. I'm tired of looking like I'm wearing a bird's nest. Also, I'd like... perhaps..."

André arched a perfectly shaped eyebrow.

"Do you think I should add highlights?"

"Come with me." André took Isabella by the hand and led her from the foyer to a black and white room of ceramic and chrome. "You'll have to trust me." She placed Isabella in a chair in front of a beveled mirror and spoke to her reflected image. "What's with the dress? Did you lose your luggage?"

"It's a long story."

"Honey, we'll have all morning. Start talking."

While Isabella replayed her journey, André removed wads of the frizzled hair.

As more hair fell to the floor, Isabella felt her mood lightening. She would be spending on this one haircut what she typically spent on hair styling in a year's time back home. But it would be worth every euro.

"I waited for the driver to return. Airport security said there wasn't anything they could do." Isabella decided to leave Scott Hancock out of the story. André hadn't asked how she'd traveled to the hotel. It was best to let the subject drop.

"Ninety-nine percent of the drivers are honest men and women just trying to make ends meet. All it takes is a few fucks," André grumbled.

Isabella shrugged. "My clothes made me look like someone's

grandmother anyway. Maybe I'll find a new style to go with my new hair."

"It'll all work out," André said.

"When can I look?" Isabella faced another stylist and his client, her back to the mirror.

"Later." Deft fingers and a razor flew around Isabella's head, sending pieces of hair flying in odd directions. "Now for the eyebrows."

"What? No!" Isabella recoiled and covered her brows with her fingers. "They're fine."

"Sure, if you want to look like you've got woolly caterpillars tacked to your forehead." André pried Isabella's hand back to her lap. "Relax."

The chair dipped back, giving Isabella full view of the recessed ceiling lights.

"André—ouch!" Isabella twisted her head to the side. "Call me a wimp, but that hurts."

"Yeah, it will. Wait a minute. I'll be right back. No peeking."

André ran from the room and then returned with ice.

"This will help numb the skin." She rubbed Isabella's eyebrow arch with a cube. "Now, don't move. But you can talk. What room number did you have?"

"Five-oh-one. The view was absolutely spectacular."

"That's my favorite room. Mario and I stayed there on our anniversary. *Semplicemente meraviglioso.*"

Isabella couldn't help but sigh. "Translation, please."

"I said, 'simply wonderful.'"

"Tell me, André, why *did* you move to Italy? If I'm prying, just ignore the question."

"You're not prying at all. It was after my divorce. I was in a bar on the Lower East Side with some friends. We were throwing darts, and I was whining about how I needed a fresh start. There was a world map on the wall. A friend dared me to throw a dart at the map and move to whatever spot I hit. The only caveat was that since I'm good at darts I had to be blindfolded. I hit Italy. Rome, to be exact. And here I am. Have been for twenty years."

"You moved to a foreign country, without knowing anyone?"

"Sure, why not?"

"Were you scared?"

"Nope. Life is about living. The marriage was over. It seemed like the perfect time to try something new. I stayed in a low-budget hotel until I got my paperwork in order. I had worked at a salon in New York, and I landed this gig. I've been here ever since."

"Ouch! But your Italian sounds like you're a native. Did you speak it before you left New York? And could you please rub some more ice on my eyebrow?"

"No problem, hon. I only spoke English. That's the best part of my story. I took a class at the university and met Mario. He teaches there. At first I wanted nothing to do with romance, but he wooed me and we got married, and now I have three fabulous *bambinos*."

"So you moved to a foreign country, met Mario, fell in love, and you're a mother."

"Well, it wasn't easy, believe me. Italian men have different ideas of how they want to be treated, but, yeah, it is like a fairy tale. He's super. And my bambinos are the bomb. Okay, sit tight. I want to bring in Juliet. Be right back." The clacking of André's heels receded while she called over her shoulder, "And no peeking."

André came back and gestured to the woman at her side. "*Questo è Juliet*." The other woman extended her hand.

"*Ciao*, Juliet."

"Actually, hon," André interjected, "we tend to use good morning, good afternoon, and so on when you meet a stranger. Try again."

"*Buongiorno*, Juliet."

"Buongiorno, signora. È un piacere incontrarti."

André burst into laughter. "You should see your expression. Priceless. Juliet only said she was pleased to meet you. Anyway, she'll be doing your makeup while I tend to my next client. I'll come back in about thirty minutes." When Isabella started to protest, André smiled. *"Rilassare. Vorresti frullato?"* André waited for Isabella's response. When none came, she sighed and said, "I just said *relax* and asked if you'd like a *frullato*?

"Excuse me. *Frullato*?

"Fruit smoothie?"

"Yes, thank you."

André's narrowed brows and crossed arms got her message across. Isabella quickly changed her response. "*Si, grazie.*"

Moments later, another salon employee arrived with Isabella's *frullato* and a sealed envelope. "*Signora*, this was delivered by the hotel concierge."

Isabella eyed the hotel's insignia on the envelope. "*Grazie,*" she said and took both items.

The envelope held her attention as she sipped the drink. Her name was written in a sweeping script on the outside of the cream paper.

"Who would be writing to me?" She slipped the unopened envelope into her bag and focused on Juliet and the cosmetic application.

"Ready, hon?" André held the back of Isabella's chair.

"I'm nervous. What if I look worse?"

"Thanks for the vote of confidence." André laughed. "You couldn't look any worse than how you already did. Close your eyes." André spun the chair. *"Uno, due, tre. Aperto!"*

"What?"

"I said open your eyes."

Isabella fell forward. A stunning woman stared out from the mirror. "André, you and Juliet are magicians." Isabella touched her hair. Golden highlights shone off short, razored pieces within a richer version of her brown color.

"Do you like it?" André asked.

Isabella ran a finger along her tamed eyebrows. And her face! "I've never felt more beautiful in my entire life."

She traced her brows, past her eyes to her lips. Juliet had enhanced her brown eyes with shades of light peach and moss green, adding a smudged line along the edge of each lid and under the lower lashes. Cheeks once pale and lifeless shone with a hint of apricot rouge, and peach gloss covered her lips.

Isabella sprang from the chair and hugged André. "I can't thank you enough."

André returned the hug. "Hey, no crying. I don't think Juliet used waterproof mascara."

After releasing André, Isabella spun and admired herself again. "Whatever this costs, it's well worth it. Even if I have to walk the streets to get more cash."

"Unfortunately, in that dress you won't get many offers, despite the great hair and makeup." They both laughed and hugged again.

"Well, let's keep in touch." Isabella bent and took hold of her bag. "I'll write my email address down if you want."

"Hey, where are you going?" André placed her hands on her hips and narrowed her eyes.

"I'm leaving. You have other clients, and I have to find a second-hand clothing store and get to the airport to rent a car."

"Oh, no. You're not putting my artwork in second-hand versions of that dress."

"But—"

"*Zitto*!" Long fingers snapped at Isabella. "Wait for me out front."

As she passed a mirror, Isabella couldn't help but glance at herself. The woman in the glass smiled at her.

A gentleman passed Isabella as she walked to the foyer. He smiled at her and whistled. *"Bellissimo,"* he said.

Instead of avoiding his gaze, Isabella called on something she hadn't known she possessed and smiled back. "*Grazie*."

André handed Isabella a slip of paper. "Here's the name of a shop I want you to visit." A sealed envelope followed the paper. "Give this note to Tony or to Gina, his daughter. They'll take good care of you. Come back here afterward."

"André, I still have to pay."

"*Zitto*!"

"What does that even mean?"

"It means to shush. Take a taxi to *Via Frattina*, number twenty. The address is on the slip of paper in case you forget. The taxi fare should cost you no more than eight euros. As soon as you get in the cab, tell the driver you won't pay more than that. Have Tony put you in a return taxi and come back here."

André swept perfumed kisses on Isabella's cheeks. "You're going on an adventure. Now get your beautiful face out of here and remember—smile, you're in Rome."

"Thank you... I mean *grazie mille*, André."

Isabella pushed against the door of the salon. Three hours earlier, she had entered one woman and was now leaving someone different. Or was she the same woman with a brighter outer shell?

An adventure André had called it. She was already on an adventure. Maybe she should just hire a taxi to take her to the airport, rent a car, and head on her way. How many adventures could one woman handle?

If she decided to leave Rome, she would need to go back into the salon and pay. Would that insult André? After all, she did need clothes. Isabella fingered the piece of paper. She would go, buy some clothes, then return, thank André, and pay the salon.

She walked up to Piero and requested a taxi.

Fifteen

A WHISTLE, shrill enough to break the sound barrier, radiated across the plaza and became part of the noises of the city. Two seconds later, a car slightly larger than a coffin screeched to a halt near Piero's legs.

Isabella settled herself in the back of the diminutive automobile and gave the driver the paper with the address.

He nodded as Isabella stated the amount of money she was willing to pay. *"Si, Signora. Va bene."*

During the drive, Isabella slid her finger under the flap of the envelope she'd received while having her makeup done. She slipped out a note card and began reading.

Isabella, please accept my sincere apology for my comments last evening. My behavior was appalling, and I am sorry. I meant what I said about finding you intriguing and that I would like to get to know you—no strings attached. I'm providing my cell number. Call me anytime.

While in Tuscany, remember to stay on the paths and keep a tight hold on your satchel.

Yours, Scott

After rereading the note, Isabella returned it to the envelope. "Now what?" His cell number offered a method of communication. Should she use it? What would she say?

She dropped against the back of the taxi's rear seat and watched as Rome zipped by.

Twenty minutes later, the taxi driver delivered Isabella in front of a brick building. Brown paper blocked the interior side of the windows, reminding her of the shut-down factory areas back home.

Nothing indicated this was *A Mia Amore*, the store name André had written on the slip of paper.

"What have I gotten myself into?" She glanced around. The location was clearly not a tourist destination. Cars flew down the street while people walked by with purposeful strides—some carrying travel mugs while others toted briefcases.

She turned the brass doorknob and entered a small room filled with the strong aroma of coffee but little else. A pretty girl sat behind a narrow desk, her attention directed at a magazine open on the desk's surface, a desk lamp the only source of light. Her dark hair fell in ringlets around her lowered face.

"*Scusami.*"

The young girl looked up and smiled. She couldn't have been more than seventeen. "*Buon pomeriggio.*"

"Do you speak English?" Isabella asked.

"Yes, I do. How may I help you?" She closed the magazine and came around from behind the desk. "I am Gina Dimitri."

"Hi, I'm Isabella Martini. André… I don't know her last name. Wait." Isabella removed the envelope from the pocket of her bag and handed it to Gina.

"André from the Hotel Hassler gave me this to give to Tony or his daughter."

"*Si*, I am his daughter." A hand tipped with neon green fingernail polish reached for the envelope.

While Gina read André's note, Isabella glanced around the room. In addition to Gina, the desk, chair, and lamp, a ceiling fan spun silently in the high ceiling. They didn't even have a computer. What kind of clothing store didn't have a computer? Or clothes?

A velvet curtain behind the desk hid what Isabella quickly assumed was a torture chamber. Except for André, no one knew she was here. The tall hair stylist could be the leader of a sex trade organization. Or the person who delivered unsuspecting tourists to the leader.

Gina stood and said, "Follow me."

Isabella called out in a panic-filled voice. "Wait. I, um… I just forgot I have an appointment. Thank you anyway, but I have to leave."

"Don't worry, *signora*. You are perfectly safe."

Gina's laugh seemed sweet and innocent, but Isabella continued to refuse. "Oh, it's not that. I just forgot I have an appointment. Thank you."

"*Signora*, you will feel better if you meet my father, yes? One moment."

Gina swept the curtain aside and vanished into the back room. A few moments later, she returned with a petite, balding man.

"*Signora*, this is my father. Antonio Dimitri."

Antonio's wide grin buried his eyes as he offered a quick bow. *"Buon pomeriggio, signora. Lo sono Tony Dimitri. Come posso aiutarti?"*

Gina spoke rapidly to her father, who nodded. They exchanged a long string of Italian, and Gina showed him André's letter. He nodded again, added more Italian, then spun on his heels and walked back through the curtain.

"*Signora*, I told my father you don't speak Italian, and he does not speak English. I will interpret." Gina walked around Isabella and engaged the front door bolt. "He is busy but can give you some time as you are *Signora* André's friend. Please, follow me."

Gina walked up to the curtain and angled her head back at Isabella. "You are coming, yes?"

Managing a fraction of a smile, Isabella nodded and followed Gina into the back room. After all, this *was* supposed to be an adventure.

What Isabella had assumed was a human trafficking center turned out to be an expansive warehouse full of merchandise. Like soldiers ready for battle, racks and racks of clothing lined the center of a room as long as a football field.

"It is deceiving, no?" Gina said. "My father, he commands an empire. Come, I show you."

They moved around the clothing racks.

"I would have never imagined this was back here. The front room is so tiny, but this… this is enormous." She was making herself dizzy from the circles she walked in. Shelving units bearing the weight of cartons, shoes boxes, and more clothing buried the entire back wall. Garage doors stood at the left end of the room while a row of mirrored doors lined the right.

Gina led her back to the curtained entrance where she noticed a glassed-in office. She counted five desks, each with a large computer and two photocopiers. A row of doors lined the wall alongside the office.

*"Si, si. Venire." T*ony waved his hand at Gina as he moved into the office.

"My father would like to begin." Gina escorted Isabella to one of mirrored doors. "There's a robe inside. Please remove all your clothing."

"Excuse me," Isabella sputtered.

"*Si*, everything. I will return in a moment."

Gina left Isabella standing in a dressing room big enough for four people. A three-way, floor-to-ceiling mirror reflected her from the front and side—all showing a woman wearing a panicked expression. She was fine with undressing but not with an audience.

"Remove my clothing?" she mumbled and fingered the silk, rose-colored robe. "Why? I'm a size ten. Just give me some clothes to try on."

"*Signora*, you are ready, *si*?"

"Um, no, not yet. Another minute, please."

Using the toe of her left sneaker, Isabella kicked off the right one, then bent and pulled off the left. Next, she peeled away the dirty shift before sitting down to remove her socks. Her arm was barely through one sleeve of the robe when Gina knocked again.

"*Signora*, now you are ready?"

"Yes. *Si.*" Isabella quickly tied the robe's sash and stepped back against the center mirror.

Gina entered first, carrying an espresso which she placed on the small table in the corner of the room. Tony came in second with a tape measure around his neck.

"Please, *signora*, remove the robe. My father, he needs to determine your size."

Isabella straightened and clutched the sash. "I'm a size ten."

"Non posso misurare attraverso la veste," Tony said to Gina, his hand waving at the robe.

"My father cannot measure through the robe, and European sizes are different from American. Please, it will be fine. He's seen many women. Even André. I will stay."

Gina guided Isabella's hands away from the robe's front and untied the sash. The silk material slipped off Isabella's shoulders amid loud clicking sounds from Tony's mouth.

"No, no. Perché le donne americane indossare tali indumenti intimi orrende?" His hands flew around as if he had suddenly become inflicted with a muscular spasm. *"No, no, no."*

Isabella reached out and grabbed the robe. What was he going on about?

Tony added head-shaking and moans. In less than a minute, she planned on taking the robe, wrapping it around herself, and running from the building.

"Gina, what's going on? Is he having a stroke?"

"My father, he does not understand why American woman wear, how can I say, puritan undergarments."

"Puritan under..."

Her white bra and matching high-waisted panties weren't Victoria's Secret quality but definitely not puritan. There was even a pink rose on the bra.

Tony looked at Gina. *"Gina , ha il suo decollare i suoi indumenti intimi troppo, per favore.*" He left the room, still shaking his head and clucking his tongue.

She didn't have a clue what he had said, but the way he said it, she knew it was a demand.

"Now what?" Isabella dropped on a hassock near the table. She raised the espresso cup with one hand while keeping the robe against her chest with the other. "Does he want me to take off my underwear too?"

"*Si.*"

"*Si?*" She almost spilled the coffee. "He wants me to remove my underwear! But, then I'll be... No, I'm sorry, but, no, I can't." This wasn't an adventure—this was torture. Absolutely not. She would not strip down.

"Tell your father I will not. I cannot."

Hoping to emphasize her determined refusal, Isabella shook her head and added her own moans. "There is no way I'm taking off my underwear. If he can't measure me with them on, then so be it. Absolutely not. Not going to happen. Nope."

She chugged the hot, thick liquid. The roof of her mouth exploded in pain.

"Do you have a ladies' room, Gina?" she moaned.

"*Si, signora*. Right next door. Follow me."

Isabella quickly donned the robe and followed Gina to the adjacent room.

"*Signora*," Gina said. "My father is a professional. You will be beautiful if you allow him to do his work. I will leave you now."

This was unbelievable. All she wanted was a few items to get her on her way. Why couldn't they throw her a dress and some socks? She'd buy whatever else she needed in *Camaiore*.

Isabella drew a deep breath to steady her nerves. So far, she had flown across the Atlantic, defeated a bully, had coffee with two handsome actors, engaged in witty and vehement banter with one of the actors, and obtained a new hairdo. Even better than all that, she had come to understand a deep-seated secret about herself. Hadn't she accomplished enough?

While she washed her hands, Isabella studied her reflection. She couldn't help it; the woman in the mirror was too attractive to turn away from. She was striking—and appeared confident. But was she confident enough to stand in front of two strangers in her birthday suit?

Tony hummed to himself as he took quick measurements. Gina held a notebook, jotting down the numbers he called out. The busy man looped the cloth tape measure around Isabella's neck, breasts, rib cage, upper arms, waist, hips, thighs—even her calves and groin. He then exited as promptly as he had entered.

"See, that was not bad." Gina revealed her pretty smile. "I will return with my father's selections."

Left alone, Isabella pulled out her cell phone and calculated the conversion for one thousand dollars. She would have to tell Gina her limit and what items were absolutely necessary—like a jacket and a pair of pants and shorts.

Gina knocked and entered carrying an armload of clothing. "*Signora*. My father, he will be back. These are for you to try."

"Okay, but I need to discuss prices with him or you, Gina. I have—"

"*Si, signora*, the prices. Let us find the clothes, then we discuss the prices."

"Gina, these clothes are beautiful but look expensive. I can't afford more than—"

"*Signora*, no worries. You are on André's account."

Isabella shook her head. "No, I just met André. She can't pay for my clothes. That's impossible and not acceptable at all."

Gina laughed. "*Signora*, André is not purchasing your clothing. It is best to let her explain the details, but I will do my best. After.

Let us now get you clothed. Here, this first."

Isabella nodded and took the bra Gina held out.

"No offense, but how is this skimpy thing going to do any good? I'm not well endowed, but the girls still need support."

Laughter burst from the young girl. "You are funny, *signora*."

"That's me, a hoot. Please, call me Isabella. After all, you've seen more of me than even I look at."

Gina continued laughing while she fastened the bra's hooks. She demonstrated how Isabella should lean forward and allow her breasts to fill the cups.

Isabella gawked. She had the most amazing cleavage. Her breasts looked stunning. "How can such a little thing...? There isn't even any padding."

"My father, he design his lingerie. He study a woman's body and movements to create the perfect foundation to the clothes he sells."

"Does he design the clothes too?"

"No. Those he buy."

"Well, kudos to him." Isabella turned and twisted, keeping her eyes glued to her chest. "I don't care what this bra costs, I want it. Actually, I want one in every color."

"Here. You need these." Gina giggled and placed a piece of lace in Isabella's hand.

Holding up the panties, Isabella noticed the cotton-lined crotch. Tony undoubtedly knew his stuff.

Without disputing the size or skimpiness, she slipped them over her legs.

"Wow!" She nodded appreciatively after performing a few squats. "Do they have glue in the bands?" They hugged her butt cheeks instead of riding into the crack. "Your father would make a killing selling these in the States.

"He does. Would you like to try this first?"

A pale yellow, cotton shirtdress with a cinched waistline and hairline white pinstripes hung innocently from the hanger in Gina's hand.

Isabella frowned at the lack of sleeves.

"Um, Gina, I don't wear sleeveless clothes." She held up her right arm and shook it, allowing the skin underneath to jiggle. "My triceps are in there, just buried."

All giggling ended, and Gina's voice took on a seriousness much too wise for a young girl. "Please try it. Your body is God's creation, and you should celebrate with him."

"I don't think God had this body in mind when he was ordering the champagne, but why not?"

Isabella slipped the dress over her arms. "This feels like silk. It must be a thousand thread."

"*Si*, the designer is expert at his fabric choices."

"Who is it? Is he well-known?" Isabella started fastening the dainty white buttons.

"No. My father helps young designers. To get them started."

"Oh, oh, oh." Isabella was stuck on repeat, unable to get the words out. The dress was exquisite. She would purchase it, no matter how expensive.

Gina reached around Isabella and fastened a narrow, white, patent-leather belt along her waist. Afterward, Isabella slipped into her sneakers.

A timid knock on the door preceded Tony's voice. "*Gina, è tutto buono?*"

"*Sì , papà . Entra.*"

"Ah, *bellissimo.*" Tony clapped his hands and spun Isabella. *Bellissimo* he repeated until he noticed her sneakers. "*No, no, no!*"

"Please, Isabella, you try on more clothes." Gina quickly led her father out of the dressing room.

It was past three when Tony finished outfitting Isabella. Two over-sized luggage bags overflowed. The final inventory included lingerie, dresses, shorts, capris, tops, pajamas, a walking jacket, and four pairs of shoes. Isabella laughed when Tony lifted her sneakers and grumbled d*isgusto,* but she managed to save them before the trash barrel became their new home.

The last items he added to the piles included a cashmere sweater, raincoat, bathrobe, and leather purse.

Tony grinned, reached out, and pulled Isabella down to his level, allowing him to kiss each of her cheeks before he waved her away. *"Devo tornare al lavoro."*

"My father, he say he must return to his work." Gina led Isabella into the front room.

"Gina, please. I can't take any of this." Isabella implored. "I need to pay."

"Isabella, we have a saying here in Italy. *'Non è importante cosa c'è sotto l'albero, ma chi c'è intorno.'* 'You accept this clothing as gifts from people God has surrounded you with.' A taxi is waiting for you." She kissed Isabella's cheeks, then opened the front door.

Isabella returned farewell kisses to Gina's cheeks. "I will never forget you and your father. *Grazie mille.*"

"*Prego*, Isabella. Safe journey."

Isabella allowed the driver to place her luggage in the trunk while she climbed in the back.

"Hotel Hassler, *grazie,*" she said when he entered the front of the cab, adding the amount she was willing to pay.

Sixteen

AFTER checking her new suitcases with the hotel's concierge, Isabella entered the Rossano Ferretti's busy foyer. She would pay the salon and André, then be on her way. If the hotel's courtesy ride to the airport took thirty minutes, and barring any mishaps with the rental car, she should be on the road by four-thirty and in *Camaiore* by nine. Her original plan of traveling along the coast would have to wait for another day.

"*Ciao,*" she said to a different, although just as beautiful, young man located behind the salon's reception desk. "Is André available?"

He smiled at her and pointed toward an empty seat. "*Sì, un momento, per favore.*"

Making herself comfortable, she accepted a glass of sparkling water from another employee and waited. Without André's kindness, she would be clothed like a pauper instead of a princess. She wished there was something she could do to repay the kindness.

"Oh, my stars! You look amazing!" André's voice carried across the room. "Stand up and twirl for me."

Isabella complied, accompanied by André's clapping. Nearby patrons and the receptionist joined in.

"*Bellissimo*," André sang out. "Here, I have a gift for you." She handed Isabella a heavy tote filled with small boxes and bottles. "Now you'll shine brighter than the Tuscan sunflowers. I'm ready; let's get out of here. *Ciao*, Alfredo." She waved and took Isabella's hand.

"Wait, André, I have to pay." Isabella pulled André against her.

"It's all taken care of, hon."

"What do you mean it's taken care of? I have to pay."

André stared steadily at Isabella. "I put your visit through a special program we have for VIPs. Your treatment today was on the house. However, if you want to tip the employees, that would be wonderful. We can discuss it at home."

Isabella resisted André's momentum. "At home? I'm leaving for—"

"I've decided it's too late for you to drive to *Camaiore*, so you'll be staying with us tonight. We have a lovely guest room, and my kids will be thrilled to have an *Americano* sleeping under the same roof." André started walking, her grip on Isabella's hand remaining firm.

Isabella pulled André back "What, whoa. I can't stay with you."

André stopped and faced Isabella. "Why not?" Her eyes widened.

"Well, because—"

"Because nothing. You're *loco*. You'll stay with us and leave bright and early in the morning. I want you to meet Mario and my bambinos. Now, stop yanking me and let's go."

Isabella didn't budge. "The *conceierge* just ordered a courtesy car to take me to the airport."

"No *problemo*." Linking her arm through Isabella's, André forced her to walk out of the salon and to the *conceierge*'s station. André spoke to him, and he nodded and smiled at Isabella while removing her luggage from behind his desk. He then reached for the phone.

"See, I told you it was all good. Now let's go. I have to stop at the market."

André gripped one of the suitcases. "I see Tony took good care of you. I can't wait to see what you got. We'll have a real girl's night. This is going to be fun."

"Wait." Isabella halted by the revolving door. "How will I get my rental car?"

"Hon, I'll drive you tomorrow. You're in Italy. Relax and go with it. And stop stopping."

André breezed through the revolving door. She turned and called out, "*Andiamo. Sto avendo compagnia per la cena.*"

Isabella struggled to keep up with André's long legs. In the past, she would have pulled away. Now, she allowed the tall blonde to pull her along the street.

"I understood *andiamo* for *let's go* and *cena,* which is *dinner.* That was about it. Italians talk way too fast."

"I said I'm having company for dinner. And if you think I speak fast, wait until you hear Mario. *Mama Mia.*"

Isabella and André walked down *via Sistina* for several blocks until André stopped alongside a white FIAT Panda.

"Put your bag on the back seat and climb in. Just push the cups out of the way."

Isabella chuckled at the collection of paper coffee containers littering the passenger floor. "How many coffees do you drink each day?"

"I'm a New Yorker turned Italian. I have coffee in my veins instead of blood." André added her own chuckle and started the car. "Buckle up."

André's driving brought Isabella to a new level of fear. Scott wouldn't have been able to compete with the darting, weaving, and lurching.

"Are you sure your name isn't *Mario Andrétti*?" Isabella called over the racket of horns and car engines.

André screeched to a halt, the tires of the car behind them squealing loudly. "Mario says I possess Lella Lombardi's soul. She was an Italian Formula One driver."

"Wonderful. How many other dead race car drivers are inhabiting the people in these cars? I'm going to get killed when I start driving in this city."

"Perhaps you have one yourself who'll awaken when you start driving."

Skidding to an abrupt stop, André swore in Italian at the driver in front of her while she leaned on the horn. "*Idiota*," she yelled out the window.

Isabella watched in shock as André inched the car forward and tapped his bumper. The driver flashed his middle finger out his window and then sped forward.

"Just remember to stay to the right and ignore the horns," André said.

"Or bumper tapping?"

"Yeah, well. New York driving habits are hard to break."

"It sounds—Watch out!" Isabella shrieked. "Why do the pedestrians just walk in front of the cars?"

André laughed brightly. "It's that interminable Italian spirit."

"Anyway, I'm not going to put you out." Isabella brought the conversation back to the next morning. "You have to work tomorrow. I'll take the train."

"Nope, tomorrow's my day off. It's the boys' last school day, and we always have a celebration."

"André, you can't keep doing things for me. This has to stop."

"Why?"

"Because."

"That's not an answer. If you really want to repay me, you read to the boys tonight, and Mario and I will take a romantic walk around the neighborhood."

The Colosseum came into view. "That's the Colosseum." Within a flash, the view retreated.

Isabella grinned. This was the same way Scott had shown her several of the sights. *Oh, that was the blah, blah* he had said as it vanished behind them.

The soft fabric of the dress slipped easily through Isabella fingers. She couldn't stop the thought from forming, nor did she want to. She wanted to think about him. Was he on his way to his villa or still in Rome? The balloon, emptied of its last remaining helium, lay safely in her carry-on bag. She knew after she returned home she would periodically hold it and remember her time with him. His attention and thoughtfulness. What would he say if he saw her transformation? Would he be attracted to her now?

"What are you frowning about?" André's voice reawakened Isabella's consciousness. "You look like you've lost your best friend."

"Actually, I've found a friend." Isabella faced the driver's seat and smiled. "You."

"I'm glad you said that. You and I, we're *anime compagna*. Sit tight. I'll be right out." André parked in front of a market and left Isabella to decipher the phrase.

Outside the window of the car, Rome's blood pulsed. Even in the suburbs, the life force of the ancient city flowed like its infamous river. Isabella closed her eyes and leaned back, allowing the scents of the urban streets to quench her thirst. A tempting bouquet layered itself into the tinge of exhaust, creating a potpourri of intoxicating aromas.

Isabella opened the browser on her phone and searched the translation of André's words.

Soul companion.

The expression was new to her. She had heard of soul mates but never a soul companion. She had to admit that meeting André had felt like meeting a friend—a long-lost friend. There was an easiness about André—a safety in the pale blue eyes.

Opening a new window in her browser, Isabella searched for the definition of soul companion. A soul companion, the website stated, is someone who shares a deep understanding with us; they're a person who is on the same emotional wavelength as us. Soul companions come into our lives when we need a teacher, friend, and companion—someone to lovingly share our journey.

"What on earth were you thinking about?" André entered the car and tossed her bag on the rear seat. "You looked like you were flying on invisible wings."

Warmth swept across Isabella's cheeks. "I was thinking how lucky I am to have met you. Thank you, André. For so many things."

"Open your voice recorder," André said.

"Why?"

"*Per amor di dio*, just do it! You can be a stubborn woman."

Isabella swiped her phone's screen and chuckled. She seemed to be hearing that quite a lot lately. "Okay. Ready."

"Non camminare dietro di me; non riuscirei a guidarti. Non camminare davanti a me; non riuscirei a seguirti. Cammina semplicemente accanto a me e sii mio amico," André recited into Isabella's phone. She ended the app and handed the phone back. "When you're lonely in your villa, listen to my words. I'll be hugging you."

André started the car. "Now let's get home. I'm dying for you to meet my boys."

Seventeen

"WE'RE less than ten minutes from the apartment," André said. "Fill me in. Why are you traveling alone?"

"It was on my bucket list."

"And?"

"And, nothing. Everyone has a bucket list."

"Don't kid a kidder, Isabella. You came into the salon looking like a haggard old woman. I don't just mean your dress and hair. Your eyes were lifeless." Since they were stopped in traffic, André spared the chance to glance over at her passenger. "Spill."

Isabella chewed her bottom lip. She wasn't accustomed to tasting lipstick. Releasing the skin, she raised one of her shoulders in a halfhearted shrug. "It's a long story."

"I won't pry. But, since you know mine…hint, hint, hint."

"As long as you keep your eyes on the road and don't get us killed, I'll give you the highlights," Isabella said.

"Deal. Shoot."

Where to begin? She could start with her father's stroke; meeting Freddy; her life with her mother—even her mother's illness. Why not start with Freddy's leaving or her mother's death? Where was the best place to start the story?

She sought the comfort of the smoothness of the ring and began. "It all started with a box."

Unlike with Scott, Isabella found herself telling André about the ring, too.

The gridlock of cars turned the ten minutes André has predicted into twenty minutes, which gave Isabella ample time to finish. André hadn't interrupted, only occasionally offering a nod.

As the cars in front of them started moving, André spoke. "Do you think your mother was married before she met your father?"

"I don't know what to think. There's no way to find out the truth."

"I get it. You're not here to solve the mystery of the box; you're here to solve your own mystery."

"Something like that." Isabella gave another brief shrug. "I want to be less of a spectator to my life. It would be nice to have an active part in it. Does that make any sense?"

André turned left onto a narrow street and pulled in to an empty parking spot. "We're here, so we'll have to continue this tonight." She turned off the engine, then shifted her entire body so that it faced Isabella. "But, before we get out of the car, let me say that I get what you're saying." André drew Isabella into a quick hug as chaos spilled out of the apartment's front door.

Three boys came barreling down the front steps.

"*Ciao*, Mam-ma," they called in unison. The tallest boy pulled open the driver's door, allowing the shortest boy the opportunity to propel himself onto his mother's lap. He clamped his arms around André's neck.

"*Ciao*, Michel." André kissed the black curls on top of the boy's head as she squeezed him in a tight embrace.

Michel stared up at Isabella through the black tendrils cascading over his forehead.

He pulled his mother's ear close to his lips and whispered none too softly, "Mam-ma, *lei è una principessa?*"

"No, *mio amore*. She isn't a princess. But she is a nice lady all the way from America. Tonight we will be speaking English in her honor."

Long black lashes encircled eyes the color of dark chocolate. Cheeks, full and rosy, formed a round face accented by a button nose and pink lips, now opened into a wide smile.

Extending her hand, Isabella stretched out the pronunciation of her introduction. "*Ciao*, Michel. *Il…mio nome… è Isabella.*"

Michel reached out. Their hands joined. "*Ciao, signora. Io sono Michelangelo.*"

They climbed from the car to the joyous outburst of a child's voice.

"*Ciao, Mam-ma.*"

André's two eldest sons stood patiently by the car.

"*Ciao, mia bambinos.*" André stood and pulled the older boys into a group embrace with Michel in the center. "Tonight we speak English. We have a guest. Come meet her."

"*Ciao, mia Isabella.*" Isabella emerged from the passenger side of the car and extended her right hand.

The boy introduced as Leonardo towered over Isabella by two inches. Neat black hair, slicked away from his forehead, framed his mother's clear blue eye color.

He bowed and said, "Welcome to our home, *signora.*"

Next came brown-eyed Federico. Black bangs hung over downcast eyes, and long hair covered the sides of his face. "It is a pleasure to make your acquaintance, *signora*," he said in a low, barely discernible voice.

"Federico is my shy one." André lifted his chin and peppered his face with wet kisses, causing him to close his brown eyes and squirm.

While Federico tried to disentangle himself from his mother, Michel tugged on Isabella's dress. "*Scusami, lo sai* Iron Man?"

"Michel, *non essere stupido.*" Leonardo lightly slapped Michel on the side of his head, sparking an explosion of Italian.

André quickly intervened. "*No, no, no. Stop, questo istante.*"

"*Mam-ma*, you say we must speak the English. Why you not?" Michel asked.

Before André could respond, Leonardo started yelling at Michel again. Isabella watched as the tiny Italian drama played out. Eventually, the older boys pulled her bags from the car while Michel collected the groceries.

"So, what do you think of my *bambinos?*" André's eyes stayed on the boys as she asked the question.

Isabella watched them disappear through the building's main door. "*Bambino* is a bit of a misnomer, but they're beautiful, spirited young men. And I could gobble Michel's cheeks."

André looped her arm with Isabella's. "I do, every chance I get."

"Which apartment is yours?"

Half-moon balconies, draped with scarlet geraniums, adorned the first two floors of the three-story building. More geraniums spilled over the roof.

"That top area looks lovely," Isabella added.

"My in-laws live on the second floor, and that's their garden. We have the first floor, and our garden is on the other side of that wall." André nodded to a brick enclosure covered with the thick foliage of a vibrant purple clematis. "Another thing Italians love, besides driving fast and good food, are flowers. We'll tuck them wherever a root will take hold."

"I thought you said your in-laws owned a villa in *Viareggio?*"

"*Si*, but they come into the city often enough. When they're not here, I have use of their *governante*."

"Government?" Isabella asked.

"Oops, sorry. Housekeeper. Come, I'll introduce you. She lives on that top floor. The one without the balcony."

Isabella followed André into the apartment. A heavily mustached woman slightly taller than a gnome greeted them with a toothless grin. Aside from a green apron dusted with what looked like flour, she was dressed entirely in black, including opaque stockings and a black hair net over heavily dyed black hair.

"*Buona evenine,* Signora *Bianci.*" The housekeeper's eyes danced from under drooped lids.

"*Buona evenine,* Luisa. *Questo è Signora Martini.* Isabella, this is Luisa."

Buona evenine, Luisa," Isabella said. "It's a pleasure to meet you."

Luisa let fly a rapid stream of Italian to which André said out of the side of her mouth, "She doesn't speak a lick of English, so just smile and nod."

Isabella was doing her best to nod as fast as Luisa spoke when Michel returned.

He took hold of Isabella's hand and tugged. "Princess, may I show you my home?"

"Go with Michel. I'm going to clean up and then help Luisa. If you need me, I'll be in the kitchen." André called out, "Federico, Leonardo, *venire tendono ai nostri ospiti*."

Isabella bent her knees and looked into the brown pools of Michel's eyes. "I'd love to see your home. But first, will you show me a bathroom?"

"*Bagno*, s*i*, Princess. Please come with me."

With her hand in Michel's, Isabella allowed him to guide her through the bright apartment. Corners and flat surfaces burst alive with flowers. Roses, lilies, orchids, sunflower-filled vases—even a flowering vine coiled around a large picture window in the dining room.

"Your *Mam-ma* loves flowers," Isabella said as she and Michel entered the guest room.

"*Si*, she love them. Each shop she buy more. The *bagno* it in there." He pointed towards a closed door at the far end of the room just as Federico came in, carrying a large vase filled with a rainbow of sweet-smelling freesias.

"*Mam-ma* told me to bring these to you, *signora*. Where shall I place them?"

"Oh, goodness, they're gorgeous. I don't know." Isabella turned. "Perhaps by the bed. That way I can smell them while I sleep. *Grazie*, Federico. Now, if you'll excuse me, I need to wash."

The bathroom welcomed Isabella with its vivid blue walls, tangerine-colored towels, and hanging basket of orange and yellow begonias. As soon as she returned to New Boston, she would visit Grasshopper's. Her new home needed flowers—and lots of them.

When she emerged from the bathroom, Isabella found Michel sitting cross-legged on the bed, his elbows pressed on his knees with his chin resting in his small palms.

When he saw her, he jumped down and ran over. "Now may I show you my home?"

"Yes, of course. I'm all yours."

The tour of the apartment started with the kitchen.

Michel explained in careful English each room's main feature. "In this room we cook; in this room we play; in this room we study." When they reached his bedroom door, he had Isabella close her eyes before they entered. "Okay, Princess, you may open your eyelids."

"This is lovely," Isabella exclaimed.

Michel crawled onto his bed and asked, "What do you like the most?"

"What do I like the most? Hm, well, let's see. There's quite a lot to like in here. I like the poster you have of Iron Man."

Isabella walked around the room as Michel watched her, a serious expression on his young face.

"I really like the color of your bedspread. Blue is my favorite color, by the way. And I like the windows. They let in a lot of sunshine. Hm, oh, I especially like your fish tank." She sat next to him and added, "I also like you. I'm glad we've met. What do you like the most about this room?"

The wheels to his childlike brain could almost be heard spinning as he pondered the question. "I like my Iron Man. I like my fish. I like my blanket. I like my windows. And I also like you."

Leonardo popped his head into the room. "Michel, *Mam-ma* needs you. *Signora*, may I escort you on a walk?"

"No, voglio portarla a fare una passeggiata!" Michel fled the room while yelling at the top of his lungs. "*Mam-ma!*"

"What was that all about?" Isabella asked.

"Michel wants to be the one to take you for a walk. However, he must finish his worksheet for school."

Isabella followed Leonardo to the kitchen and into the heat of André and Michel's squabble.

"André, may Michel come with us? I promise we'll make it a fast walk."

"See Mam-ma, we will walk fast. We will run." Before André could argue, Michel grabbed Isabella's hand and pulled her to the front door. "Come, Princess, before *Mam-ma*, she say no."

Federico bolted to catch up while shouting goodbye to his mother.

Isabella kept hold of Michel's hand as he skipped along beside her and his brothers. They walked the remaining length of *Via Icilio* and turned right, eventually reaching *Largo Manlio Gelsomini,* an expansive, cobblestoned square. Stores and restaurants edged a multi-lane road.

Isabella stood still and inhaled. The odor of diesel from the passing buses clung to the remnants of the day's heat. Far from being offensive, the scent drew her in. Garlic and spices from the many restaurants lining the road added their own brand on what was becoming Rome's signature fragrance in her mind.

A brightly painted kiosk silently invited Isabella to sit and drink a *frullato*. A shrug and quick shake of her head refused the offer, but she tore off a tiny piece of herself and deposited it on the plaza, as if she were Gretel leaving crumbs to mark the trail back home. Someday, she would return.

"I don't want your mother to be angry with me," Isabella said. "We should start back to the apartment."

"*Si*." Leonardo pointed to an adjoining park. "We will walk through there and come to the street."

Michel burst into a run to chase a flock of pigeons while the rest of the group followed behind.

The walk back along *Via Icilio* seemed different to Isabella. The plaster of the buildings took on more vibrant shades of their pastel beauty. The peach tones brightened; the rose shades deepened; and the creams brightened to an ethereal height. The trees shading her pulsed with life. She heard, smelled, and saw everything. It was as if a second heart formed within her—sprouting from her core and beating to the rhythm of Rome.

When they returned, André ushered Michel to his room and told Federico to take Isabella out to the patio.

Federico led the way to a round table, with a top built from a mosaic of artistically patterned tiles. After opening a green cloth umbrella, he entered a small storage shed and returned with seat cushions. Placing one on each of the chairs, he said, "Please, *signora*. Sit."

"Only if you call me Isabella."

His tanned skin turned a shade of rose that rivaled the peonies.

Isabella smiled and sat. "You call me whatever you like, Federico. *Grazie*."

"Would you drink water?"

"Si. Grazie."

Left alone on the patio, Isabella drew in a deep breath. Though it wasn't quite six, the sun still hung high enough in the sky to keep the air warm.

"*Scusami*." Federico returned with a tall glass filled with bubbling water, garnished with fruit. He set the glass carefully on the table and placed a green cloth next to it. "I return soon," he said and scrambled back into the apartment.

Italian music drifted from a neighboring apartment window and combined with the sounds from within André's apartment. Someone out on the street called out a name. A horn tooted, and a woman on the opposite side of the garden wall laughed. Isabella closed her eyes and leaned back and listened to the orchestra surrounding her.

"*Grazie*," Isabella called after him.

A faint whistle called behind her. Isabella turned to see a small bird, proudly displaying a vest of yellow feathers, singing happily from a rose bush.

"That is Luigi." Leonardo arrived with a stack of plates. "Michel feeds him."

Leonardo called through the door before he started distributing the plates, depositing one in front of each chair. Federico arrived with cloth napkins and utensils, followed by Michel, who settled on the patio floor.

The bird hopped onto Michel's shoulder, then into his hand and pecked at the seeds he carried as he started singing, "*Stella stellina; la notte si avvicina, la fiamma traballa; la mucca é nella stalla. La pecora e l'agnello, la vacca col vitello; la chioccia coi pulcini; la gatta coi gattini; e tutti fan la nanna nel cuore della mamma!*"

Isabella leaned forward and kept her voice at a whisper. "Michel, what do the words mean?"

An angelic voice responded. Isabella turned to see Federico's eyes closed as he sang, "Star, little star; the night is coming; the flame flickers; the cow is in the stable. The sheep and the lamb; the cow with her calf; the hen with her chicks; the cat with her kittens; and they are all asleep in the mother's heart!"

"Federico sings in the church's choir," Leonardo offered, beaming with pride.

A man's voice called from inside the apartment. "*Faccio a sentire un canto angelo?*"

"*Pap-pa!*" Leonardo and Federico rushed inside. Isabella and Michel remained on the patio, Michel with his bird and Isabella in her seat.

André's husband, Mario, walked out, flanked by his two sons.

He ruffled Michel's hair, then directed his attention to Isabella.

"*Buonasera*, Isabella. I am Mario." A noble face smiled at her. Beneath the kind, brown eyes sat a long, straight Roman nose, thick mustache, and narrow chin.

He approached Isabella's chair. After the customary kisses to her cheeks, he added, "I welcome you to my humble home."

Isabella stood. "*Buonasera*, Mario. Thank you for having me as a guest."

Mario's height barely brought his forehead to her shoulder. Obviously, Leonardo and Federico inherited their height from André. But their hair color was all Mario's. His slicked-back hair glistened in the sun's rays, the gelled ebony curls tight against his scalp.

"Please, sit." Mario moved to the opposite side of the table and pulled a chair outside the range of the umbrella's shade. "The sun feels good. I cannot get enough."

"André tells me you work at the university?"

"*Si*, I teach there. Tell me, how are you enjoying my fair city?"

"I love it," Isabella responded and took hold of her water glass. She hadn't meant to emphasize her reply with so much enthusiasm. "I can see why André fell in love with Rome. It has a way of getting into a person's blood."

André arrived with a tray laden with wine glasses, wine, a plate of crostini, assorted cheeses, and pickled olives.

"Isabella, this is Mario." André moved and encircled her husband's broad shoulders. She had removed her hair from the ponytail and a sheet of silk tumbled over her husband's chest. "*Il mio amore.*"

"We met, *cara mia*. It seems our guest has fallen to Rome's charms."

"*Fantastico*." André clapped her hands. "Move here, Isabella. It would be the balls. You can stay with us, and Mario can teach you Italian."

"Whoa, slow down," Isabella said. "I'm sure other people feel like this when they travel to a new place."

"Sure they do, but you're not other people. Just say you'll think about it."

"Okay, I'll think about it." Isabella laughed. André's avidity was contagious, and if she didn't watch herself, she just might stay, and that would lead to a phone call from hell. Hello Beth, I'm not coming home. Beth would launch a military extraction.

Before they continued, Leonardo shouted, "*Mam-ma*, *Zio Scott è arrivato*."

"*Scuzie*." André kissed her husband, then left the patio.

Eighteen

ISABELLA shot from her chair. She might not be able to speak the language to save her life, but she did know a few words, and *arrivato* meant here. Scott was here—at André and Mario's house. He had to be stalking her. He'd probably followed her, and André and was now making some excuse why he was at their door. The only exit, beside the apartment's front door, was through the gate in the front of the garden—which would land her directly in Scott's path. What could she say to Mario that would explain her sudden need to flee over the back wall? She'd left the stove on?

"Isabella, please, what is bothering you?" Mario was at her side, handing her a glass of wine.

Laughter carried from the front road as a car engine revved. Leonardo shouted something in Italian and Scott's voice responded, after which both of them burst into more laughter.

Her stomach muscles, relaxed a second ago, were twisting into a knot. "I'm...I'm just feeling a little queasy. If you'll excuse me, Mario. I need to...excuse me."

Isabella fled to the safety of the guest room. She seated herself on the bed and wrung her hands. The mirror in front of her reflected her new haircut, still made-up face, and her eyes—presently filled with panic. From the shouts and laughter, Scott apparently knew the family. How on earth could he know a hairstylist and language professor? What was up with him? Did he know everyone in Italy?

"Isabella." André's voice spoke low and clear. "May I come in?"

"Yes," Isabella called out.

André entered. She wore a sheepish grin while she leaned against the edge of the bureau. "Hm, perhaps my plan was *folio*."

"Your plan?" Isabella looked up at the woman she had only met that morning. "What plan?"

"Let me explain. Scott came into the salon after you left. Told me about this woman he'd helped who was staying at the hotel. He was hoping to see her again after she got settled in *Camaiore*. I put two and two together and drew my own conclusions. I wanted you to come and stay for the night, so I insisted he come for dinner too." She cocked her head. "But now, based on your expression, I feel I've made a mistake."

"I don't understand. Why would you invite Scott Hancock to your home?" Isabella asked.

André settled next to her and clasped one of her hands. "Scott seemed so enamored with you. He didn't mention that you and he had a problem."

Isabella removed her hand from André's and stood, claiming the spot André had just vacated. She didn't know what to do with her hands. They wanted to run through her hair and tug, but the curls were long gone. The best alternative were the buttons on her dress.

"No, you'll pop them off!" André reached out and took hold of Isabella's hand. She pulled her back onto the bed's edge. "You'll ruin your dress. Why are you upset? Please tell me."

"What did Scott say about me? What did he tell you, exactly?"

"Well, he mentioned that you lost your luggage and that he took you out for dinner and gelato. And, as I already told you, that he was hoping to see you again."

"He didn't mention my behavior?"

"No." André angled her face to look at Isabella. "What behavior? Spit it out."

"It's nothing." Isabella shook her head. "I'll explain later. What does *zio* mean? Leonardo said *zio* Scott."

"It means uncle. Listen, I have to get out there, but I want to explain something first. How much do you know about Scott Hancock's background?"

"Well, I know his mother was Italian and his father British. He told me she died of lung cancer and his father a heart attack. He was born in Italy, and after his parents divorced, his father moved him to England. He's been married once and is a famed womanizer."

"Don't believe everything you read. As for the first part, *si*, that's all true. Scott grew up in the villa next to Mario. His mother was a famous opera singer and my mother-in-law's closest friend. The boys were like brothers when they were young. After the divorce, Scott got whisked away to Surrey and placed in a private school. He spent school vacations at the villa, where he and Mario were inseparable. I suspect you read the parts about him being a womanizer in the tabloids. Scott's not that way at all."

"Wait. You're telling me Scott Hancock is some celibate hermit?" Isabella scoffed.

"Not completely. He is a grown man. And a handsome one at that. According to Mario, Scott embraced the life of fame as any person might. He basked in the attention. Unfortunately, things didn't go so well for him, but I'll let him explain that part. After his divorce from Julia, he pulled back. He's actually low-key. Loves to read. Enjoys conversation. Has a great sense of humor—very dry. He's wonderful with the boys, and they love him and see him as their uncle."

André hugged Isabella. "I need to get back to my family. Stay in here if you'd like."

She stood to leave when Isabella asked, "André, does Scott know I'm here?"

"No. I wanted to surprise you both."

Isabella chuckled. "Well, you've certainly taken me by surprise."

André held onto the door's edge and faced back into the room. "Don't hide, Isabella. You were brave enough to travel far from home to find yourself. What's a few more steps?" She turned and pulled the door closed.

Isabella remained on the bed. Scott didn't know she was here. Would he be happy to see her? After all, she had reamed him pretty good last night.

Isabella walked to the bathroom and freshened up. The one toiletry she didn't have was a fragrance. Tomorrow, she would buy herself a spritz of some sort. Something light and floral. André said that Scott was hoping to visit her in *Camaiore*. How would he have even found out where she was staying? Oh right; he knew every man, woman, and child on the continent. Probably Sicily too.

"Princess, may I enter?" Michel's sweet voice called into the room.

Isabella smiled and almost skipped to the bedroom door. "Of course you may enter." She swung open the door.

"Please, you will come and meet my *Zio* Scott. He is funny and said he would like to see you. Please, Princess. You will come?"

How could she say no to such an innocent request? "Yes, Michel, I'll come meet your *Zio* Scott. Let's go."

Scott's attention was directed at Mario, the two men deep in conversation. When he glanced up and saw Isabella, he shot out of his seat, an expression of disbelief and then immense pleasure covering his face. His eyes fixed on her. He made to move in her direction but stopped.

"Isabella."

She knew he would do it before it happened. His hand moved through the shorter salt-and-pepper waves. "I...You look smashing. But why...?"

"You two. You know one another?" Mario asked. "How is that so?"

André interjected. "I'll explain later, *mio amore*. Come help me in the kitchen. *Bambinos*, come with Mam-ma and Pap-pa. *Pronto*." She clapped her hands rapidly and ushered everyone from the patio, leaving Isabella and Scott alone.

Neither one spoke. Rather, they stood staring at one another.

Scott walked up to her. The patio started to spin, and Isabella felt herself teetering. She had to apologize. Before anything else happened, she had to say she was sorry.

"Mr...Scott, I—"

"Isabella, I—"

They each interrupted the other. Scott said, "I'm sorry. Ladies first."

"No, please. What were you going to say?"

"I..." He stroked the back of his neck and chuckled. "Bloody hell, I seem to have lost my train of thought."

Isabella smiled and lowered her head to the side. "Then I'll go first. I'm sorry for my poor behavior last night. I...my insecurities are no excuse..."

"Stop." Scott moved closer and took hold of Isabella's hands. "Stop. Don't say another word. It is I who needs to apologize. You shared your story with me, and I only thought of how I might fit into it. I never stopped to realize you might not want me to be part of it. I acted like a fool. Forgive my selfishness."

Isabella gazed into Scott's face. The last time she had seen his eyes, the color threatened of an impending storm. Now, the gale had passed, and she was looking into a soothing pool of gray. His words didn't make any sense. Last night he had said...but now—

André and the boys returned. André carried a large bowl of seasoned olive oil and several small dishes while Federico carried a platter of antipasto; Leonardo, a tray of glasses; and Michel, a basket of bread. Mario followed with another bottle of wine.

Each person took their seats. Before eating, Mario offered a prayer of grace and opened the wine. Glasses were filled. Isabella listened in amazement as the children talked at once. The ancient language flew back and forth into a finely woven web, enclosing the family in a tight knit of love. Only she and Scott remained silent.

Mario clapped his hands and quiet settled over the patio. "We are forgetting our guests. Please, Isabella, tell us about yourself."

Isabella had been about to bite a piece of *prosciutto* when all eyes focused on her.

André laughed. "Way to put her on the spot."

Michel's round eyes focused on Isabella. "I will ask you a question, please, Princess?"

"Yes, of course, Michel."

"Why you wear the husband ring on the different finger?"

"I'm sorry." Isabella looked from Michel to André.

"I think what my *bambino* is asking is why do you have a wedding band on your right hand?" André glanced at her son and added in a stern tone, "Although he knows better than to ask such a personal question."

"Please, André, it's okay." Isabella looked at Michel and smiled. "I'm not married, Michel. The ring was my mother's."

"Why she no wear it?" Michel asked.

"*Abbastanza*!" Mario shouted. "That is enough, Michel. You embarrass our guest."

"Mario," Isabella implored. "He isn't embarrassing me. He's just a child, and he's trying to understand." Facing Michel again, she said, "It helps me think of my mother."

"She is back in the Americas?"

"She..." Isabella stopped speaking. How was she to explain death to a young child? What if Mario and André hadn't had reason to ever discuss it with him?

Scott came to her rescue. "Michel, Isabella's *Mam-ma* is with the angels. Just like *Nonna Bianci.*"

Michel nodded thoughtfully and asked, "Is your *Mam-ma* knowing my *Nonna*?"

Isabella nodded. "I'm sure they're good friends."

Michel slipped from his chair and walked around the table to Isabella's side. His small hands reached up and cupped her cheeks, the innocent eyes full of a wisdom that only resides within a child. "You may stay here, Princess." Rising on his toes, he kissed her cheek, after which he asked, "*Mam-ma*, when we have ravioli?"

Everyone laughed, and Mario raised his glass for a toast. "To our new friend, Isabella. And to my *amico*, Scott. You do us an honor by sharing our table. *Alla tua salute!*"

"To your generosity, Mario," Scott replied.

Isabella added, "Thank you for inviting me to stay in your home."

Her glass and Scott's touched edges as a chorus of voices joined in a single *salute*.

Nineteen

ISABELLA stood on the empty patio and watched the darkening sky. A faint crescent moon peeked from behind a wisp of a cloud as the sun concluded its decent. Solar lights blinked on, giving the patio an ethereal appearance. In the distance, someone was listening to the music of Frank Sinatra. At present, Scott and Mario were in Mario's office, André and Luisa were cleaning the dishes, and the boys were having their baths. Isabella had been told to relax.

Dinner had passed without any further inquiry into Isabella's personal life. Scott had entertained them with stories of stunt mishaps and injuries he'd received during the filming of *The Inspector.* How he'd had to wear a protective cup because he kept hitting his groin while jumping into a car and that he'd actually punched the actor playing his movie adversary, cutting his knuckles on the man's teeth.

There was an ease about Scott, Isabella reflected. The man at the dinner table, the one who showed immense pleasure in making the children laugh, pulled her deeper into his orbit. She couldn't escape his words from last night, though. The humiliation she'd felt at his rejection still stung. And how was she supposed to blend that comment with the one from tonight? How he'd wanted to be part of her story? None of it made any sense. Instead of finding answers to her life, thus far this trip had opened up more confusion.

"I would say the caterpillar has finally come out of her cocoon."

A jacket slipped over Isabella's shoulders as the British accent reached into her thoughts.

"Excuse me?" Isabella angled her head to face him. She wanted to believe she drew the jacket's edges across her chest because of the cooling night air, but it had nothing to do with the temperature. The scent on the fabric aroused a yearning she found delicious yet frightening.

Isabella searched Scott's eyes. If they would only reveal some hint as to what words she should believe.

"I said, the caterpillar has finally come out of her cocoon," Scott repeated.

"Yes, I heard. I'm confused why you said it."

"Your appearance. You've taken my breath away with your new wings."

Isabella bristled. "So now, Mr.—"

"I swear, Isabella..." Scott's hair became the destination for his hand, his fingers sliding through the remnants of the waves. "If you call me Mr. Hancock one more bloody time..."

"Fine. So now, Scott, you're attracted to me? All it took was a new hairdo and a pretty dress?"

She snickered and looked across the patio at the fountain. Arriving at its side, she focused on the pale lights lining the inside edges of the granite. They turned the water into a fluid rainbow although the beauty did little to assuage her regret at her comment. Why was she constantly striking out against this man? If she didn't want anything to do with him, she should just tell him. Unfortunately, that was the problem. She did want something to do with him.

"Ah, this dance again. Fine." He shrugged and added, "Maybe I find you fascinating."

Isabella turned and faced Scott. "I'm a woman from a small, rural town in New Hampshire. Not many people would call me fascinating."

"Perhaps they haven't looked deep enough. I tell you what: let's play a game."

She reached in and teased the tinted water droplets. Coins layered the bottom of the basin, and she wondered if the children used the fountain for making wishes. If she were to make a wish, what would it be?

"I'm not in the mood for a—"

"Humor me, would you?"

"What sort of game?"

Scott strode up to her and pulled her back from the fountain. "Stand here and look at the water in the fountain. What do you see?"

Isabella watched the colors play on the surface of the water. "I see water."

Scott kept his hands on the sides of Isabella's shoulders. "Excellent. Now, let's move closer. Right up to the fountain."

Scott guided her to the fountain's edge. "Right here. Now tell me what you see?"

After releasing a quick breath, Isabella said, "I see sparkling coins."

"Outstanding." He leaned close to her ear. "That, my dear, is how I see you. Below your quiet depths, you sparkle."

With a flick of her wrist, Isabella sent a stream of water onto the patio.

"All well and good, but a person isn't a pile of change resting on the bottom of a fountain. A person comes with their past, and sometimes the past makes the water murky."

"Ah, but if the coins sparkle bright enough, they'll penetrate the murkiness."

She turned and gave Scott a puzzled look. "What do you want from me, Mr.… Scott? Please don't get me wrong. I truly appreciate your help, but for goodness' sake, you're a celebrity."

After he inserted his hands into his pants pockets, Scott shrugged and said, *"Se cammina come un'anatra, e fa qua qua come un'anatra, deve essere un'anatra."*

"The King's English, please."

"If it walks like a duck, and quacks like a duck, it must be a duck. I'm an actor therefore, you assume, I have an agenda. What about you? What's your agenda? You could have told me to piss off."

Scott stopped and scratched his jaw. "Actually, come to think of it you did. However, it wasn't convincing."

Isabella held the edge of her bottom lip between her teeth. Eventually, she said, "Yes, but you were more than convincing last night." She added, her voice quivering, "I believe you said you weren't attracted to me."

Scott chuckled while moving closer. "I believe I said, and I quote, 'When did I ever say I wanted to bed you?' It's not a good idea to mix words with a performer. We have great memories."

Stepping to the side, Isabella began to leave, but Scott held onto her arm. "Please don't walk away. This time I shan't follow."

"*Signora* princess, *mi volete leggere una storia*?" With André in hot pursuit, Michel ran onto the patio and threw himself against Isabella's legs.

"I'm sorry. He got away from me." Michel held onto Isabella while André tried to pry him off. "We'll be out of your way in a moment. *Michelangelo, venire subito. Pronto*."

"It's okay, André. *Ciao*, Michel." Isabella bent down. "What did you ask me?"

"*Mam-ma* she say you may read me a story?"

"I was going to collect on my payment." André continued her tug of war with her son. "Mario and I are going for a walk, and it's time for Michel's story. But I see you two are talking, so I'll have Luisa read to him."

"Nonsense." Isabella held her hand out for Michel. "I'd love to read you a story. Let's go."

With Scott's jacket still draped over her shoulders, Isabella and Michel walked hand in hand toward the patio door.

Michel ran back and took Scott's hand and pulled him along. "*Zio* Scott, you may listen too. Princess is reading tonight."

Scott grabbed Michel and tossed him in the air. "Listening to Princess read would give me immense pleasure." He ran into the apartment with Michel bouncing over his shoulder, giggling with glee.

Isabella started to follow, but André stopped her. "So, how's it going? That jacket looks stunning on you, by the way."

"Great. Your family is lovely. I'm so glad—"

"Right. I'm mean with our Mr. Hancock." She tossed one of the suit coat's sleeves and added, "I see my plan worked."

"Your plan might just backfire."

"Never underestimate the power of a New Yorker slash Italian. We have tricks up our sleeves you can only fantasize about." André tossed the sleeve again and released a confident laugh.

Twenty

THE elder boys were already in their beds. Federico lay under the blankets on the bottom bunk while Leonardo sprawled across the top bunk, each lost in their own books.

Scooting under his blanket, Michel called to Isabella, "*Mam-ma* she sits here. You may too." He patted the spot next to his pillow.

"Okay." Isabella rested against the headboard, allowing Michel to nestle under Scott's suit coat. "What story do you want me to read?"

"An American story."

"An American story? Do you have a book of American stories?"

"No, Princess. Please, you tell me one."

"Let me think." She could always tell him the story of the spinster from New Boston. Laughing to herself, Isabella decided against it. The twists and turns had her head spinning. Imagine what it would do to a six-year-old. "Okay, I have one. One day..."

"*Scuzie*, princess. But you must begin with once upon a time."

"He's right, you know," Scott said from across the room. He'd chosen Federico's bed, his head currently propped against the boy's bent legs. "All good stories begin with once upon a time."

Isabella drew in a shaky breath and started anew. "Fine. Once upon a time, in a field of sunflowers on a Tuscan hill, a mother deposited a tiny egg to the underside of a green leaf."

"How tiny was the egg? As tiny as a *granello*?" Michel asked.

"Hm, I don't know that word."

"Speck," Leonardo called down from the top bunk. "It is a speck."

"Okay, good. The egg was as tiny as a *granello*," Isabella responded. "And round."

"What color was it?"

"Michel, *smettere di fare domande,*" Leonardo demanded. "He is asking too many questions."

"It's fine, Leonardo. I don't mind." Isabella noticed the older boys had closed their books and were paying attention to her story. "The color, well, what color do you want it to be?"

"*Giallo*," Michel announced.

"*Stupido, Mam-ma* she told you to speak the English."

"Leonardo," Scott said. "If I have to speak to you once more about calling your brother stupid, you and I will go out onto the patio to have a talk. Apologize."

"Si, *Zio* Scott. *Mi dispiace, Michel.*"

Isabella snuggled close to Michel and whispered, "What does *giallo* mean?"

"Yellow," he mumbled, clearly embarrassed by his brother's castigation.

"Alright, a yellow egg." She added a kiss to his curls and continued. "As days passed, while rain fell, and sunshine warmed the leaf, the yellow egg grew until, one day, it hatched."

"And Iron Man came out!" Michel shouted.

"Michel, ferro l'uomo non può andare bene all'interno di un uovo. Tu sei un imbecille," Federico yelled. Leonardo added his own comments until Scott intervened.

"Enough," he shouted and silence resettled on the room.

"*Zio* Scott, he is angry," Michel said.

"Yes, Zio Scott does seem to be angry. Let's keep going with the story, and perhaps he'll be happy again," Isabella replied. "Let's see, where was I? Oh, yes. The egg hatched, and, no, Iron Man did not come out." She kissed Michel's forehead, then continued. "A small caterpillar came out. She was also very *giallo* and very hungry. On her first day out of her egg, she ate a large leaf. The next day, she ate an entire apple. On day three, she ate—"

"A plum," Michel called out.

"Okay, a plum. On the fourth day, she ate...what do you think Federico? What did she eat on the fourth day?"

"I don't know. A sneaker." They all laughed at the ridiculousness of the suggestion.

Isabella braced herself for another outburst from Leonardo. When none came, she said, "On the fourth day, she ate a sneaker. A very old, dirty, smelly sneaker. That night she had an unhappy tummy. No more sneakers for me, she cried. On the fifth day, she ate... Leonardo, it's your turn."

"A pizza."

Michel flung his arms against his bed. "A caterpillar, she can no eat pizza."

"It's fine, Michel," Isabella said. "This little caterpillar can. So, on the fifth day she ate a whole pepperoni pizza, and she spent a second night with a very unhappy tummy."

"Give *Zio* Scott a chance," Federico said.

"My turn. Let's see. I've got it. On the sixth day, she ate a sunflower."

Isabella enjoyed the way his accent played with the words. She paused to savor them a moment, then began again. "By now our little *giallo* caterpillar wasn't little any more. She was a fat caterpillar. She didn't understand what was happening to her. She wasn't hungry anymore, and she felt funny. This has been a great life, she thought, but now it is over. I guess I must die."

"No!" Federico murmured.

"But Princess, she cannot die." Michel knelt in front of Isabella. His brown eyes pleaded with her to change the ending.

"Just wait. Be patient and listen." Isabella held her arms open and Michel let her wrap them around him. "The yellow caterpillar said a farewell to the hillside where she had lived. She said farewell to the sunflowers and the birds and the rain and the sun. She built a barrier between herself and the world and accepted her fate."

Leonardo sat up and shouted down into the room. "A cocoon. She's isn't going to die. She made a cocoon!"

Isabella smiled and winked at him. "Many months passed. Wind howled and snow fell. One day, while the sunshine warmed the nook in which the yellow caterpillar had built her cocoon, she woke up. Why, I'm not dead, she thought. But I do feel strange. How do I get out of here? She pushed and nudged against the walls of her chamber until it cracked. It wasn't easy, but she managed to pull herself free. Looking at her body, she stared, amazed at what she saw. Two shriveled wings, the color of the sky, were attached to her sides. Well, these are new, she said. She crawled away from the cocoon and rested on the tree's bark, allowing the sun to warm her."

"Oh, please, Princess. May I say the ending?" Michel pleaded.

"Yes, of course. Go ahead."

"Her wings they opened, and she became a *bella farfalla,* and she flew into the air and lived happy ever after. The end."

"Meraviglioso." André and Mario clapped from the doorway.

"We only managed to hear the end, but that sounded like it was a *magnifico* story. Now it is time for sleep," André said.

After kissing each child, Isabella said goodnight.

When she walked by André, she said, "I'm going to take a shower. If you have time, I'd love to talk."

"Give me twenty minutes and I'll be in. Would you like tea or wine?"

"Tea, *grazie*." Isabella walked to the guest room.

Mario called from the hallway. "Isabella, we will be having wine. Join us."

"*Grazie*, Mario, but I'm going to take a shower and prepare for bed. It's been a long day."

He nodded. "Then I'll say *buona notte*."

"Buona notte to you too." Isabella closed the bedroom door

and looked at her reflection in the mirror. She toyed with the ring as she considered the woman in the glass. Scott's jacket still hung from her shoulders. She should join the others and give him back his coat. Sure, that was a sorry excuse to see him again, but it was all she had.

Isabella removed Scott's jacket and placed it neatly on the bed. How could she want to see him when all she did was flail in denial when he came near? It was as if the frothing ocean of life she'd damned up with such expert precision suddenly threatened to burst free. What then? Would she sink or swim?

"He's sleeping here!" Isabella stumbled out of the bathroom. "Excuse me!"

"Not here, here." André bit into the edge of a chocolate *toto*. Wetting the tip of her index finger, she used it to collect the crumbs on her lap as she added, "He is upstairs in my mother-in-law's guest room. It didn't make sense to send him back to the hotel when he'll be driving you to the airport. I forgot I have a meeting at Michel's school. I hope you don't mind." André swallowed the last piece of a cookie.

Isabella removed the bathrobe from the suitcase presently lying on the bed. After slipping into the soft cotton sleeves, she tied the sash and then helped herself to a cookie. "Mm, these are scrumptious. Now, back to tomorrow. Why do I get the feeling this is another part of your plan?"

"I would love to take credit, but it was Scott who insisted. He's driving up the coast, and the airport is on his way."

"I can take the train. It'll give me a chance to get a flavor of traveling like an Italian."

"Nonsense. You'll lose your beautiful clothes and luggage."

"What is it with everyone thinking I can't hold onto my luggage?"

"Your track record speaks for itself. Now, sit still for a bit, drink your tea, and tell me why you're running from Scott."

"Who said I'm running?" Isabella lifted the second suitcase onto the bed and undid the zipper. "Do you want to see what Tony selected for me?"

"You're changing the subject and yes, I do." André leaned forward and yanked a silk blouse from Isabella's hand. "Answer my question first. You told me about your mother's box, the book, and plane ticket. Even the ring. Now finish the story. What are you running from?"

"The ring. Wait. Hold on. The ring. Princess. André, that's it!"

"What's what?"

Isabella fished in her carry-on bag for the book. She then pulled a pen from the side pocket of the bag. "I had a dream last night. About my mother and...anyway, in the dream my mother told me to remember the name she used to call herself when we played the princess game. It was Gina. Princess Gina Conti." Isabella wrote the name onto the inside cover of the book.

"I'm lost."

"I am too. But it's important. I just don't know why."

André narrowed her brows. "You started to say your mother and then stopped. And who? Scott?"

"Seriously, André, has anyone ever told you you're relentless?" Isabella laughed and lifted her tea cup.

"*Si*, one of my finer qualities." One of the perfectly shaped eyebrows lifted into an arch. "So, are you going to tell me or force me to beg?"

Isabella pursed her lips and shrugged. "It's not something I can tell easily... or quickly but I'll try. There was a boy... well, now he's a man...."

André sipped her tea and remained silent as Isabella struggled with her story.

"You see, I met him in high school. I was shy and he was determined. We dated… and I registered at the same college as him and we continued to be a couple throughout college. Not an exclusive couple, mind you. I thought we were, but I found out later that wasn't the case. He lived in Manchester while I was in New Boston with my mother. He would visit on weekends. Sometimes he'd skip a few. I'd call, but he'd be MIA. The short version is, he got tired of my mother and moved away… D.C. to be exact. He got married two weeks later."

"The *bastardo*." André sprang off the bed and pulled Isabella into a tight grip. "Your young man should rot in hell."

"André—"

"No, you listen to me. He had to be seeing the other woman while he was with you. He's the worst kind of man. He is no better than *una schifezza*."

"Okay." Isabella chuckled. "I'll bite. What's *una schifezza* mean?"

"It means crap. Your man is crap. *Merda. Cacca.*"

"That last one I know." A lump rose in Isabella's throat. She coughed and swallowed a mouthful of tea. "But you don't get it. I used him too."

Isabella was surprised to see André's blue eyes open in a surprise. "I'm not being one hundred percent truthful." She drew a long breath, held it for a second, and then forced a deep exhale. "You see, I've come to realize something. Actually, Scott helped me in that regard. Freddy was tired of my treatment of him because I clamped on to him. I didn't want to be alone with just my sick mother. I wanted someone to take care of me while I took care of her. But, more importantly, I treated him with contempt. I didn't respect him just as I didn't respect myself. I blamed him for our problems when I had an equal hand in the process."

After a quick shake of her head, André stated her disagreement. "Why? Because you wanted someone to care for you? We all want to be loved and cherished. That's not using, Isabella. That's being human. And we all take people in our lives for granted. That's human nature too. I have an idea. Stay here." André held Isabella's hands in a tight grip. "You can enjoy the sights of Rome, and I'll help you heal."

"André, you've given me more than I can ever repay, but this trip is something I need to do. Let's call it my quest."

"So, you're Don Quixote, and the sunflowers are your windmills."

"Something like that."

"Isabella Martini, you're a strong woman," André said. "You've broken from your cocoon, just like the butterfly in your story. Stomp the damn remains with the heel of your shoe, then fly—soar. But promise to come back and see me."

She kissed Isabella's cheeks. "I have already told you, we're *anime compagna,* you and I. Our paths are intertwined. Now show me what Tony chose for you. That dress today was stunning on you. Was Gina there?"

While Isabella unpacked one of the suitcases, she described meeting Gina and the shock she'd felt when Gina told her she had to completely undress. She mimicked Tony's outburst at her bra and panties.

"I swear; this trip is pushing my comfort zone right into the outer limits. There I was, stark naked, with this bustling Italian shoving a measuring tape into each nook and cranny of my body. I hope he disposes of them when he's finished." She and André laughed so loud they had to cover their mouths.

"Tony's a dear. He's measured parts of me I didn't know needed measuring," André said.

Isabella removed each piece of clothing and André added enthusiastic responses.

"What does Tony do, actually?" Isabella asked. "How does he stay in business? He didn't even charge me, which we need to talk about, by the way. Gina said to discuss it with you."

"He merchandises for up-and-coming designers and markets out-of-season clothing and accessories to department stores across the world. Mario's parents were Tony's patrons when he was getting started. Mario and I are Gina's godparents, and he's Leonardo's godfather. We're all one big happy family, you might say. Mario and I help to fund his many fashion shows, and in return, he keeps me well clothed. And now, you too."

"I would have thought Scott would be a godparent." She blurted out the statement without thinking about the direction the conversation would head.

André pulled her hair from around her neck and stared at Isabella. "Scott's Michel's godparent. When I gave birth to Leonardo and Federico, he wasn't dealing well and buried himself in his career. We didn't see much of him."

André moved into a long stretch as she reclined against the cushioned headboard. "As long as we're on the subject of Scott, you never fully answered my question about why you keep pulling away from him."

"I thought I had." The dress Isabella had been slipping onto a hanger slid from her fingers.

"*Menare il can per l'aia,*" André rattled off.

Isabella picked up the dress. "English, please."

"You're leading the dog around the barnyard."

"Great. That makes perfect sense. I had better luck understanding it in Italian."

"It means; you're beating around the bush. Stalling. Come on, spill. You like him. I can tell. And, by the way, he's completely smitten with you."

"What makes you say that? I'm a nobody compared to the type of women he dates."

"*Tombola!* Now we're getting somewhere."

"And to*mbola* means?"

"Bingo. Scott's life frightens you. Which makes perfect sense. It would be hard to be his lover and not get swept into the frenzy of the paparazzi craziness. But he'll protect you."

Isabella avoided André's scrutiny and focused on rehanging the dress.

André pressed further. "I told you, don't believe everything the paparazzi prints about him. Scott tired of the glamor glitzy pussies a long time ago. After his divorce, Scott rarely went on dates."

"I would be foolish to not be concerned about his life, but that's not why I pull away." Isabella sighed. "It's..." She let her sentence trail off, choosing instead to finger the delicate embroidery on the dress's bodice.

"Could it be you're afraid Scott will leave you just like that fuck Freddy did? Or you'll cling to him as you did with Freddy?" André added.

Isabella hung the hanger in the empty closet and then returned to the suitcase for lingerie and shoes. She knew she was getting ahead of herself. For goodness' sake, she had only met Scott yesterday. Besides, he was a player. Wasn't he?

"Hon." André pressed on the shoe Isabella held. "Learning to trust again is difficult. You can't spend the remainder of your life living your past negative experiences. Life is about living. Learning to be vulnerable. Learning to trust."

André stood and wrapped her slender arms around Isabella. "Part of the process is learning to trust yourself too." She ended with a tight hug.

It felt as natural as breathing to hug André back.

"*Buona notte,* Princess."

"*Buona notte,* André. And *grazie mille.*"

Twenty-One

"YOU'RE staying at a stranger's house? Are you insane? This trip has made you completely brain dead!"

Isabella chafed at the insult. She had only wanted to tell Beth where she was, not get into another battle. "Please refrain from the biting criticism."

"Do whatever you want. It's your funeral."

"I think you're overreacting. They're nice and have helped me quite a bit."

"Isabella, you're a foolish woman who's made a string of foolish mistakes in her life. But this takes the cake. Anyway, I'm cooking supper."

"What do you mean you're cooking supper? It's only four-thirty your time."

"Well, I'm starting early. Bye."

Beth disconnected the call, leaving Isabella to stare at her phone. She was a foolish woman who'd made a string of foolish mistakes. Really? Well, not anymore.

Isabella pressed redial. Beth's voicemail connected immediately.

"Beth, I know you feel you can say whatever you want to me. It's my fault. By remaining quiet, I've given you permission. Perhaps that's one of the mistakes you're referring to. From now on, you don't get to call me stupid or say other hurtful things. Hopefully, we can talk about this when I get home. *Ciao*."

Another sleepless night. Although soft and comfortable, the bed in which Isabella tossed had become as hard as a rock. A quick glance at her phone told her dawn would arrive in less than four hours. It seemed pointless to stay and thrash. She pulled on her bathrobe and padded out of the guest room and into the kitchen.

The sleeping inhabitants of the quiet apartment remained oblivious to her nocturnal movements. She poured herself a glass of sparkling water and slid quietly onto the patio. The scent of evening primrose floated on the cool night air, welcoming her to its nighttime domain. Although the solar lights had waned, the fountain continued to cast its glow, revealing their location. Isabella placed her water glass on the patio table, then walked cautiously toward the flowers, as if too quick a movement might break the spell they cast. She bent forward to take in a lungful of the aroma.

"Breathtaking, don't you think?"

The voice came from the opposite side of the fountain. The startling realization she wasn't alone quickly moved aside and made room for delight. She found herself smiling at the tall man who walked out of the shadows.

"Yes, they are."

"I apologize if I startled you."

"I have a strong heart. It can take it."

"No doubt. Care to join me?" Scott gestured toward a nearby bench. "Unless I'm intruding. In which case, I'll leave you to your private musings."

"I'd love to join you." She noted the raised eyebrow and laughed. "Does my response surprise you?"

"Very much. I fully expected the opposite. I must say, however, I'm pleased." Scott wiped at the surface of the bench and patted the area. "Do you often walk about in the dead of night?"

"It depends on my demons. Sometimes they dance and other times they lie peacefully and let me sleep. What about you?"

"I don't sleep. Not much anyway. A quick snatch here or there but, well, it's been many years since I've slept through the night. My demons are a rambunctious lot."

Scott became silent, and Isabella allowed him his solitude. He leaned back and stretched his legs, his scent melding with the primrose.

"Who are your demons, Isabella?" he asked.

Isabella exchanged a breath and reclined with him. "Remorse... loneliness... a bit of guilt... a whole lot of regret."

"Ah, yes. I'm well acquainted with those particular devils."

Eventually, Scott blew out a mouthful of air. "I was young. Just starting out in movies, after having spent a few years performing on the stage. I met Julia, and three years later we married. By then I'd made a few pictures, and my name was becoming known. Fame has a way of changing people. I worked hard to keep myself in check but Julia, she embraced it."

Running his hand through his short waves, Scott turned his eyes on Isabella. "I'm not making excuses, mind you. I enjoyed the perks that come with fame. Still do. We were living in California. Had a townhome in L.A. and a house in the southern part of the state. On the coast."

Scott fell silent. The shadows played on his features as his eyes held Isabella's.

"I hope you understand I'm not the man I play in the movies."

"You mean you don't jump off buildings or shoot people?" she chuckled.

A quick laugh matched hers. "Not if I can help it."

"Good to know."

"What I'm trying to say is that I fall prey to poor judgment, just like everyone else. I make mistakes."

Isabella furrowed her brow. "Of course you do; you're human. But I don't understand—"

"I'm sure you know the story. About Willem's death."

"Yes. I'm so very sad for your loss." Isabella remembered how sad she had been when she'd learned of Scott Hancock's two-year-old son dying in a car accident.

Scott nodded. "Thanks. What you won't know are the details." Scott withdrew his handkerchief and wiped at his eyes. After clearing his throat, he added, "It was my doing."

"I don't understand. From what I read, your wife had been driving."

"Yes, but, you see, we were in the process of filing for a divorce at the time and didn't get on very well. We were at a party and had a row. She left the party in a blaze of anger. I could have stopped her, but I let her go. Glad to be rid of her. Fate played me a cruel hand. I kept her but lost my son. Willem was home with the nanny. Julia went to the house and gathered him and headed to the beach house. She was driving there when they crashed. She blacked out. Still doesn't remember a bloody thing."

Isabella reached out. She wanted to hold him and comfort him. Her hands fell to her lap. "You do know it wasn't your fault."

"One might argue otherwise. I could have stopped Julia. Kept her at the party. But I didn't. However, if I wanted to keep living, I had to come to terms with my hand in the outcome. Don't mistake me. There's not a day that goes by that I don't miss the hell out of my son. Forgiving and forgetting are two entirely different matters, aren't they?"

Isabella slowed her breathing. She had been so caught up in her own whirlpool of emotions she hadn't stopped to consider Scott would have his own. She had been seeing him merely as a performer, when all along he had been showing her glimpses of himself. No wonder he felt the need to explain he was human.

"Scott, I'm sorry—"

"Ta, no pity," he growled. "I didn't tell you because I want your pity." Scott straightened and started to walk away.

"If you would let me finish instead of jumping in and interrupting me, you would learn I'm trying to apologize for myself."

From a few feet away, he turned. "How does it feel to have someone cut your words off?"

Isabella walked over to Scott and arched her head back. "You are, without a doubt—"

Scott slipped his arm around her waist. "Go on."

"Tell me, if you're so wise, why don't you sleep?"

"Well, I'm not bloody perfect, am I? Until then, I'll be one of the night's children."

Isabella released a soft chuckle. "You definitely should look into playing a vampire."

"Perhaps I will."

Scott moved closer and took hold of Isabella's chin. "You are a fascinating woman, Isabella Martini." He ran the pad of his thumb over her lips.

Isabella knew he felt the shiver that passed through her from the way a smile played on his lips.

He leaned in close and brought his mouth within a hair's breadth of hers. "And enchanting."

Scott closed the gap between them and claimed Isabella's lips. Years of loneliness shattered as she explored the sweet depths of his taste.

Twenty-Two

THE morning at the Bianci's house was bedlam, which reached a fevered pitch when Isabella walked into the kitchen. The boys raced to her, each clamoring for a chance to hug her and talk about the coming day.

"*I bambini, danno la povera donna po 'd'aria.*" André clapped her hands, and the children instantly stopped shouting. "They're excited, as you can tell. Michel, you may go first. Tell Isabella about your day. In English, please, my sweet."

"Princess, today is the last day of the school. Tomorrow I begin my summer." He started jumping and singing until André ushered him out to the patio. "Please place this silverware on the table."

As Leonardo and Federico collected glasses and plates, they explained their exams were today, and then summer would also begin for them.

Luisa handed Isabella a *cappuccino*.

"*Grazie*, Luisa," she said and followed the boys.

Leonardo and Federico each talked over the other, explaining their impending tests while Michel continued to sing his celebratory song. Scott's arrival kicked the frenzy up a notch.

"*Buongiorno a tutti.*" He leaned down to give each family member a kiss on their cheeks.

He came round the table and settled into the chair next to Isabella. "*Buongiorno*, Isabella," he said as he leaned her way. "Did you sleep well?"

A backdraft exploded within her, inflaming her skin. Was it possible to combust under one's own heat? she wondered. If so, with the levels filling her veins, she might end up destroying the entire block of apartments on *Via Icilio*.

After she'd left Scott a mere three hours earlier, Isabella had found respite in a brief period of sleep. Although the dream she'd entered had turned into an inferno.

She'd found herself and Scott in unknown surroundings. The walls of a small room, with hazy light filtering through a sheer window curtain, enclosed the narrow bed on which they lay. A ceiling fan spun lazily. With each pass of the fan's blades, a breeze licked their naked bodies, caressing them in the blades' steady rhythmic breeze. Instead of pulling away, she'd given herself to him, falling into him as desire coursed in her blood.

Her skin reached for Scott's fingertips as he played his hands over her, light and feather-soft, as if a butterfly fluttered against her breasts. Wherever his fingers touched, a fire blazoned.

"Please," she begged. "Be gentle. It's been so long I don't know if..." Her words melted into his kiss.

"Trust me, Isabella. I won't do you harm."

Emotions, long-ago encased and buried, pushed through the depths of their tomb.

The velveteen surface of Scott's tongue traced the length of her neck. She arched her head, allowing him full access. He traced the edge of her collarbone and kissed the small cavity formed by the bone's joining before beginning his descent along her breast bone.

She groaned with desire. Passion clawed within her, demanding release. She pulled at him.

"Patience, lass. You've waited far too long to rush, and I've no place I'd rather be," he whispered, reaching for her hands and bringing them above her head. Scott forced her fingers around the iron railings of the bed. She'd gripped the cold metal, threatening to bend the bars.

"Isabella, Isabella." He said her name as if it was a prayer.

Isabella snapped to attention. To her horror, multiple sets of eyes focused on her. Had she been moaning? She looked at André, who wore a wide smile.

"Isabella, we're waiting for your answer," André said.

"I'm sorry. I didn't get much sleep last night. What did you ask me?"

"Princess," Michel said. "You will stay. Yes?"

Isabella looked at André, who wore a wry smile on her red lips. André's wink sparked an onslaught of heat across Isabella's face. "I'm sorry. I don't understand what…"

"Please, *signora*." Leonardo added. Federico nodded his agreement, his cheeks flushed pink.

"As you can tell," André said, "my *bambinos* are enamored with you, Isabella. The boys asked if you'd stay for one more night? To join us for the beginning of their summer vacation? We always head into the heart of the city for a celebration."

Isabella looked at Scott. She stared at the gray eyes, alive with his grin. A quick replay of last night's kiss rushed into her blood. She found herself at a loss for words.

"I… I have to pick up my rental car."

"Wow! You are in a brain fog. Scott said he'd drive you to get the car, then follow you back here."

"I don't mind. I've no agenda for the next four weeks," Scott added.

Isabella looked at the children and laughed. The quaint suburb of Rome shouted louder than the call of Tuscany. The sunflowers would wait.

"Yes, I'd love to stay another night."

Michel's upward momentum sent his chair into a backward tumble. "*Grazie*, Princess." He ran at Isabella and threw himself into her arms. "We will have much fun."

"*Tempo di scuola*. We won't have any fun if you're late for school. Michel, *pronto*."

Michel rushed at Scott, flinging himself onto his lap. "*Ciao, Padrino.*"

Isabella held André in a fierce embrace. "You've saved me."

She said goodbye to the boys, ending with Michel. "I'll see you later, alligator."

The family spilled into the apartment, leaving Isabella and Scott behind.

When she noticed Scott watching her, she smoothed her dress and sat back in her chair.

"What does *padrino* mean?" she asked.

He angled toward her. "Godfather. How are you today?"

"I'm well." Isabella kept her focus on her fruit salad.

"How did you sleep? Any demons?"

"None that I can remember." She stabbed a strawberry with her fork and looked at Scott. "You?"

"Like a *bambino*." He slid the strawberry off her fork and held it to her lips.

Isabella held her napkin under the berry and bit into the red flesh.

Scott finished the remaining portion and grinned. "We have to be back here by two. Until then, I'm all yours. What would you like to do today?"

"I thought we had to go to the airport."

"I was thinking about that. Since I'm staying as well, I'll drive you in the morning, and you can follow me up the coast. That way I'll be sure you arrive safely."

"Rescuing me again, Mr. Hancock?"

"Hm, I'm being perfectly selfish. I want to spend time with you, Miss. Martini. So, I'm at your service. Any place you'd like to visit?"

The excursion Isabella had in mind sprang to her lips. "I'd like to throw a coin in *Trevi* Fountain."

"So, there's a heart of a romantic in you. Good to know." Scott stood and held out his hand. "Ready?"

Before they entered the apartment, he paused by the patio door. His arms held her against his chest. "I apologize for not saying this earlier. *Si guarda radiante, signora Isabella*."

A breathless Isabella said, "English, please."

"I said you look radiant."

He surrounded her mouth with his and delivered a lingering kiss to her lips.

When Isabella entered the guest room, she found a white, cross-body satchel lying on the bed with a note resting on top.

Isabella, thank you for giving us another night. If I have any say in the matter, you'll soon be living in Rome. Ciao, A.

Isabella peeked inside the creamy leather pouch and found a lipstick, compact mirror, and perfume spritz. She sprayed the air and walked through the cool mist. A scent akin to orange blossoms enveloped her.

She walked into the bathroom and brushed her teeth. Next she slid off the cap of André's gift, revealing a shimmering tube of coral. Edging the compact open, she applied the lipstick, then appraised herself in the full-length bathroom mirror. Isabella had fallen in love with the dress she now wore as soon as Gina had held it up. From the emerald green fabric to the peek-a-boo bodice, it made her feel like a siren from the nineteen-fifties. The princess seaming flattered her figure by hugging her curves in long, simple lines.

When she stood to the side and surveyed how she looked from the back, a grin formed on her lips. "Thank you, tout driver."

Inserting her money and passport into the satchel, she slipped it across her chest, collected her carry-on bag, and met Scott at the front door. Isabella had to admit he looked mighty fine in the tan slacks and white, short-sleeved, button-down shirt.

"Ready?" he said.

"Yup. Let's go. Oh, darn, wait. I need a coin." Isabella dropped her carry-on bag to the tiled floor and started riffling through the pockets.

"Isabella, I have a coin. No need to get yourself worked up."

Scott bent and reached for her elbow. "If you're coming back here, why are you bringing your satchel?"

"What if we get into a car accident?"

He took hold of the bag's strap and slid it onto his shoulder. "How will this hideous bag save us?"

"First off, my bag isn't hideous. And for your information, it contains what's left of my connection to home."

Scott flashed his perfect teeth. "Unless, of course, you make Rome your home. Then you can dispense with your baggage and move on."

"It's not baggage, and I think we should move on from this conversation."

"Right-oh. I'll place your stunning bag in the boot. Unless you need access to it while we're driving."

"No. Thank you. I'll be fine."

Isabella followed Scott outside. She reached for the passenger door handle, but Scott raced forward to grab it. "You American women are all about woman's lib. Give a bloke a chance, will you?" He opened the door and bowed as she sat down.

"*Grazie*."

"*Prego*." Scott closed the door, placed Isabella's carry-on in the trunk, then bounded around the car and vaulted over the door, landing smoothly in the driver's seat.

"I take it that's the move that required a jock strap?" Isabella added a smile and laughed. "What if you had missed just now?"

"I'm a pro. I'll teach it to you, if you'd like."

"No, thank you. I'm good with getting in a car like a normal person."

Scott shrugged and started the car's engine. "Your loss." Pressing the gas, he shifted into first gear and they flew down *Via Icilio*.

Twenty-Three

THE drive to *Trevi* Fountain took them along the Tiber River and eventually to *Piazza Venezia*. By the time they reached the famed heart of Rome, Isabella had found a comfort level with the way Scott confidently wove through traffic. She managed to keep her eyes open except when a motorcycle cut in front of the car. Her lids clamped shut, and she refused to open them, even when Scott told her to 'stop being such a big girl's blouse.'

"What on earth does that even mean?" she shouted over the horns and screeching tires.

"It means you're acting like a wimp. Open your bloody eyes."

"Then say I'm a wimp. For goodness' sakes, you Brits have the screwiest way of saying the simplest things."

Scott swore in Italian as he sped past the truck. "Let me remind you I'm not a Brit. I'm Italian."

"Fine. It's still screwy."

When they reached *Venezia*, Isabella watched in fascination at traffic that seemed to be coming from all directions, much of it heading right for the people trying to run to the safety of the pavement.

"How do the tourists not get run over?"

"Italians don't like to kill tourists. It hurts the economy. By the way, that..." Scott pointed to the large statue of a man on a horse in front of the *Il Vittoriano*. "is in honor of Italy's first king, Victor Emmanuel II."

Isabella laughed. "You and André should open your own business. Whirlwind Tours. Your slogan could be 'Don't blink or you'll miss it!'"

"If you decide to give me a few days in Rome, I'll take you on a leisurely investigation of all the secrets she has to offer. Agreed?" Scott cast a look Isabella's way before snapping his attention back to the road.

Having the top of the car lowered did little to cool Isabella's flamed reaction to his devilish grin. She patted her face with her fingers. Screw the coin. She might just throw herself into the fountain.

They raced onward, cutting through small streets until they arrived in an alley. Scott parked behind a van and turned off the engine. "One moment. I'll be right back." He leapt from the car and walked through the open door of a restaurant's kitchen.

Isabella heard people shout greetings to him as cooking aromas eased into the alleyway. Even though she had just eaten breakfast an hour earlier, the gurgling of her stomach almost drowned out the sounds of the city.

Scott returned alongside a short man with the muscles of a weight lifter. "Isabella, this is Luigi. Luigi, this is Isabella." Scott opened her door and extended his hand.

"*Ciao*, Isabella. *Sei una bellezz,*" Luigi said.

"Hey, no flirting," Scott kidded. "Luigi is going to let us park here while we visit *Trevi*." Scott threw Luigi the car keys and grasped Isabella's hand.

Isabella pointed to the trunk. "But, my bag."

"Don't worry. It'll be perfectly safe. We shan't be gone long."

Luigi called out, *"Bel sorriso per il paparazzi."*

Scott continued walking and waved over his head, Isabella's hand clasped in his.

"What did Luigi say? About the *paparazzi*?" she asked.

Scott looked at her and grinned. "He said to smile pretty."

The alley led to a pedestrian-filled sidewalk that rimmed a narrow street. With Isabella's hand still in his, Scott navigated them into the queue.

"You're lucky you came this summer," he said while they wove past brightly clothed tourists. "Last year the fountain was closed for renovations. Cost two-point-four million US dollars, but she's a beauty once again. Down here."

He pointed along a street. They walked around a group of people trying to take a selfie using a long, metal stick with a cell phone attached to one end when a woman called out, "Hey, you're Scott Hancock."

Isabella noted the quick, almost indiscernible tightening of Scott's hand as he stopped and grinned. The woman came running over. She brandished the selfie-stick as if it were a weapon. "Can I have your autograph?"

Soon Scott got pulled into a sea of people waving all manner of writable surfaces in his face—papers, maps, purses. One young woman slipped her shirt off her arm and offered him a pen, thrusting her exposed upper arm in his direction.

Isabella stood to the side and watched, enamored by the way he conducted himself. His grin never wavered as he endured photos and hugs from people he didn't know and would never see again.

He looked up, made eye contact with her and grinned a different type of smile—one more intimate. Speaking to the crowd, he said, "Thank you, but I really must be off." After receiving several well wishes, he walked up to her and held out his hand. "Shall we?"

They walked on and Scott said, "When we reach *Trevi* Square, just smile. And don't panic."

Isabella stopped and rooted herself to the sidewalk. "Why would I panic? What's going to happen?"

"You'll see. Come on. I'll protect you."

"From what?" She refused to budge. "Tell me first."

"There may be cameras. But if you act like it's nothing, you'll be fine. Just smile your beautiful smile and stay with me."

"Cameras?"

"Cameras. Ready?"

"No."

Spectators milled around them. Scott stood close, his face angled close to hers. "Take a sec if you need it. You might as well get used to it."

"Why? Why would I need to get used to cameras?"

"Because, my *bella farfalla,* you'll be with me, and I tend to attract cameras. It's part of the package. A part I hope you'll be able to handle."

Isabella drew a prolonged breath with hopes it would steady her pounding heart. "I… I don't understand."

Scott edged closer and arched his forehead until it touched hers. "It's my hope, Isabella Martini, that you'll want to continue to spend time with me. As you can see, I, at times, attract attention. What do you say?"

A slip of paper and a pen entered the space between them. Scott signed the paper and handed it back, never taking his eyes off Isabella. He reclaimed her hands and asked, "Does spending time with me appeal to you, despite the commotion?"

The sun beat down on the speck of earth where Isabella stood. Like the butterfly in her story the previous night, she welcomed the searing heat, allowing it to warm her still damp wings.

She nodded and exhaled. "Let's do this."

As predicted, they entered the square around *Trevi* Fountain and a band of camera-toting people pointed to them and ran in their direction, the clicking of shutters becoming deafening. Scott continued walking, leading Isabella toward the fountain, grinning as he moved.

"Just remember, they're doing their job. Smile."

Isabella felt she must look like a cat about to be run down by a car. The smile plastered on her face became an inanimate and forced entity.

The crowd in front of her and Scott parted, allowing them

access to the fountain while a man shouted Scott's name from behind. Scott guided Isabella up to the iron railing. The sound of the fountain would have been deafening had her heart not managed to drown out the roar of the falling water.

"What do you think?"

"I think I'm going to hurl," she responded.

Scott released an unrestrained laugh. "You wouldn't be the first person to barf in *Trevi*. Here you go, little girl." He placed his arm around her shoulder and handed her a one-euro coin and then turned her so she faced the crowd. "Make it count."

He stepped back, his body offering protection from the crowd.

Isabella closed her eyes and blocked out the people, the cameras, and the noise—everything except Scott and Rome. She inhaled their energy, made her wish from the depths of her soul, and tossed the coin over her right shoulder. The crowd watching them exploded into applause. A few women came over and hugged her while men clapped Scott on the shoulder.

An older man brandishing a large camera asked them to pose in front of the fountain, to which Scott obliged. He slipped his arm around Isabella's waist. She didn't know where to look as more cameras pointed their way. She finally looked up at Scott. He responded by bending forward and planting a kiss on her cheek. "You're doing great. Let's get out of here."

"But you didn't throw your coin."

"I've no need for wishes. Let's go." Taking her hand again, he started to move them away.

Isabella stopped. "No. You need to throw a coin, or my wish will be negated."

Scott cocked an eyebrow and stepped forward, the small furrows between his eyebrows deepening. "Where did you read that?"

Raising her chin, Isabella grinned. "I didn't. I just made it up, like my mind. Throw the bloody coin, Mr. Hancock."

He kept Isabella in his steady gaze as he pulled another coin from his pocket. "My pleasure, Miss Martini." Taking her hand, he led them back to the railing.

This time Isabella stood in front of Scott. "Make it count, little boy." The coin sailed through the air amidst more cheers and flashes.

"Now." Scott reached for Isabella. "Let's go."

While they raced up the sidewalk, Isabella asked, "How do you do this? Wherever you go, people want a piece of you."

"It comes with the job." He shrugged but kept walking. "I enjoy what I do, and it's part of it."

Isabella stopped and yanked him to a halt. "But wait. Why didn't the *paparazzi* hound you at the airport? The only people who bothered you were a few fans. Even in the café. Not one *paparazzi*."

"Ah, yes. Well, Clooney was landing at Gate One." Scott tugged her to start walking.

Isabella stopped again. "George Clooney?"

"Yes, now walk." Scott drew her to his side. "George Clooney."

"They wanted George Clooney over you?"

"It appeared so."

They walked a few steps until Isabella stopped again.

"This is a rather annoying habit you have, this stopping thing," Scott said. "Now what?"

"I'm going to be on the rags."

He ushered a loud laugh. "Not a good way to put it, if you understand the British use of the word rag."

Isabella realized what she'd said and released an embarrassed snicker. "Oh, sorry. I meant I'm going to be on the tabloids."

Scott lowered his eyes to hers and asked, "Does that upset you?"

"Well, at least I look better than yesterday. Maybe they won't print them. I'm a nobody."

"You, Isabella Martini, are not a nobody." Scott reached out. He took her by the waist and moved her forward again. "And, yes, they will care. Scott Hancock with a beautiful woman. They eat that stuff up."

"Well, my beauty, as you call it, is all André's doing. She should get credit in the photos."

This time Scott stopped. "André just cracked open your cocoon. You were the *bella farfalla* that emerged."

Isabella returned Scott's gaze. Butterflies. At the moment, a large flock fluttered in her blood.

Scott grinned. "You suddenly have a peekish look about you. Hungry? I don't want you fainting."

"*Grazie*." Isabella returned his grin. "I appreciate your thoughtfulness."

"We're drawing quite a gathering of admirers. Let's get out of here." Scott kept his arm around Isabella's waist and pulled her onward. "Excuse us, would you?" he called out as they moved past the shouts and reaching hands. They turned down a less crowded side street.

"You move fast," Isabella said.

"Shall I slow down?"

"No. I'll let you know if I need you to."

Scott stopped again and, using the back of his fingers, stroked Isabella's cheek. "Are we discussing walking or something else?"

The quake that exploded through Isabella's body took her breath away. Forty-eight hours ago, her biggest hurdle had been flying to Italy. The most exciting excursion she'd imagined accomplishing involved walking to a quaint shop from her villa and selecting a ripe tomato and bottle of wine. Now she was in the arms of a man with eyes that could enter her soul? It was as if she had been blindfolded, spun around, then spun again. Her eyes were open, but the vertigo remained.

"It's just that—"

"Pardon the interruption, but here's an idea." Scott pulled out his phone. "Let me make a call, and we'll talk during lunch." He swiped his phone's screen and dove immediately into a conversation.

Isabella nodded. Italian flowed, and Isabella could hear the person on the opposite end of the call matching the speed and fluidity of the language.

While she waited for Scott, a slender girl came over and extended a booklet and pen. "*Scuzie, signora, Posso avere il tuo autografo?*"

"I'm sorry," Isabella said, adding a quick shake of her head.

The girl pretended to write on one of the book's pages. "*Autografo.*"

Isabella's eyes couldn't have opened any wider at her shock. "You want my autograph? But..."

Scott continued his conversation while he motioned with his hand for Isabella to sign the book.

"Okay." She shrugged and signed her name.

"*Grazie, signora.*" The girl handed the book to Scott. After she thanked him, she skipped down the street.

Isabella released a low chuckle. "That was bizarre." By now Scott's conversation had ended, and he reached for her hand.

"Why do you think that young girl wanted my autograph?"

"Because, you're beautiful and with an actor. She obviously assumed you're famous as well. No harm. You made her happy. Well done, I'd say."

They reached the alley where Scott had parked the car. "I'll have someone run and get the car. Do you need to use the facilities?"

"Please, yes." She followed Scott into the back of the restaurant and into the dining room.

"Up those stairs, there," he said. "I'll meet you back here."

After she finished, Isabella washed her hands and then reapplied her lipstick.

Not wanting to keep Scott waiting, she reached for the bathroom door. The thought, *not wanting to keep Scott waiting,* tumbled within her brain like a rock in a clothes dryer. She drew back her hand for a moment. Giving her head a little shake, she smiled at the thought and headed for the stairs.

When she saw Scott, her lungs flipped. He stood by the bottom step. In one of his hands, he held the handles of a large brown paper bag. A trio of woman stood speaking to him. He looked her way and flashed his charming smile.

"Excuse me, ladies, I must leave. It was an absolute pleasure meeting you." He kissed each cheek in turn, leaving a trail of blushing faces. He extended his hand toward Isabella. "This time I'll take you through the front door, like a civilized person."

"I thought we were having lunch?" Isabella turned her head. The cozy establishment retreated as Scott directed her through the door.

"We are." He held up the bag. "It won't do a'tall if I hide you in a pub. Plus, I want to show you something." Scott stopped and placed the bag on the sidewalk. "Unless you want to stay." His hand began an ascent toward his hair. "I say, I'm not sure what to do."

Isabella grabbed the strong hand before it reached the salt-and-pepper waves. "Mr. Hancock, I don't really care if we eat here or on the street. But, please, let's eat someplace. I'm about to faint from low blood sugar."

"Can't have that, can we?" Scott slid his arm around her and pulled her against him, his lips a hair's breadth away. "It's a shame you put on your lipstick. I would have liked to kiss you. That might revive you for a bit." He released her and picked up the bag. "Shall we?" They walked around the side of the building to find his car waiting in the alley, the top already lowered, the keys in the ignition. A young boy stood nearby and grinned as Scott handed him several euros.

Isabella teetered on the brink of losing consciousness, but it had nothing to do with low blood sugar. The reason watched her with gray eyes as he opened the passenger door.

"Buckle up." Scott handed Isabella a bottle of water and then closed her door. He placed the bag on the back floor and jumped into the driver's seat. While he turned the key in the ignition, he said, "No closing your eyes. Agreed?"

Like a sleek panther awakening from its slumber, the engine of the black rocket purred. Scott shifted into first gear and the car eased out of the alley toward the main road.

Isabella shook her head as she chugged the water. After most of it was gone, she said, "No, I don't agree."

"Wrong answer." Scott gunned the engine and Isabella felt another one of Newton's laws come to life.

Twenty-Four

"ISABELLA, you have to blink at some point. Your eyes look like dinner plates."

She had hoped her sunglasses would hide her eyes-wide-open expression. No good. Scott saw through the sides.

"You told me not to close my eyes," she kidded.

Scott reached over and took hold of her hand. He placed it on top of the stick and covered it with his own. "This will give you something to focus on. Can you drive a stick?"

Isabella gave up and squeezed her eyes shut as she shook her head. The drivers of the other cars were beyond anything she'd experienced thus far. Cars looped, cut, screeched, and blared along the route.

"Open your eyes, luv. We'll be fine. Focus on the shifting and see if you can try to decipher the gear I'm in. There's five, but I'll only be using four. Not enough road to use the fifth. What gear am I in now?"

"Um, I don't know. First. Second, No, wait. Third?"

"Well done. Keep it up."

Scott had been correct. Calling out the gears as he shifted helped alleviate her angst. However, the problem of her getting behind a steering wheel and onto the roads still remained. "Fourth, second, first," she shouted with an edge of hysterics. "I'm going to die when I start driving."

"No worries, just remain on the right of the road. We're almost there." Scott veered to the left, pushing the gas pedal to propel them through a yellow light.

They entered *Via della Navicella,* and Scott slowed the car. A line of tour buses waited like sentinels along the tree-lined street bordered by an expansive brick-and-wrought-iron fencing.

Scott drove on and brought the car to rest in a small parking area. "Welcome to *Villa Celimontana.*" He leapt from the car and was at Isabella's door, his hand extended her way. "Come, let me show you one of Rome's gems."

Scott left Isabella staring at the statues of two women gracing the sides of the entryway while he opened the trunk. "This is amazing. How old is this archway?" she asked.

"Some historians say the 17th century." Scott returned with a green blanket draped over his shoulder. He held Isabella's carry-on and the paper bag he'd gotten at the restaurant.

"May I carry something? You look pretty burdened."

"You get this." He handed her the blanket. "But keep a hand free for mine."

They entered the garden and walked down the path. "That building there is the original villa. The Italian Geographical Society is housed there now." Scott nodded toward a three-story structure. The original rose tone of the stucco had faded to a blush pink, but the splendor of the villa remained. "We can stop in if we have time. We're actually close to André and Mario's home."

As they neared the villa, Scott directed them to the left. "I used to come here with me Mum. You, Miss Martini, are the only other woman who has joined me on these hallowed grounds."

"Get out of town."

"I kid you not."

"I'm honored, Mr. Hancock."

"As well you should be, Miss Martini." Scott laughed and swung Isabella's hand around his waist, forcing her arm against his shirt while he looped his arm around her back.

They followed the packed gravel and dirt path until they reached an opening with a tall obelisk in the center. At the top rested a concrete globe.

Scott nodded and said, "Legend suggests the globe contains the ashes of Augustus."

"What about vandals? If that were in the States, the globe would have been long gone."

"Scoundrels are everywhere, but most Italians guard their history with a fierce determination." Scott pointed toward the right. "We'll settle this way. Over by that wall."

Aged bricks topped a waist-high concrete barrier framing the area. Every twelve inches or so, ancient stone basins filled with flowers decorated the top of the wall. When they came to a spot where the wall curved, a spectacular view of southern Rome lay before Isabella.

"Where are we, exactly?"

"We're on top of *Caelian* Hill." Scott pointed off in the distance. "André and Mario's home is over there, on *Aventine* Hill."

Scott retrieved the blanket and spread it on the wall before coming behind Isabella and sliding his arms around her. He rested his head on her shoulder. "Like it?"

"I can't begin to explain what I'm feeling right now. I… I want to consume this city. Eat it for breakfast, lunch, and dinner. I want to drink in its flavors and sounds. I want someone to inject me with its beauty so it will become part of me."

Scott's laughter vibrated through her body. "One would say you're doing a bang-up job of finding the perfect words. Ready to eat, or do you want to feast on Rome a bit longer?"

Isabella arched her head so it rested against Scott. "I'd love to feast on Rome. However, I don't think I'd last very long. Let's eat real food."

Scott released her and began removing the bag's contents—a small loaf of bread, a wax-paper-wrapped section of salami, another package containing a chunk of pungent cheese, a hard-boiled egg, and two brightly polished red apples.

"The traditional feast calls for wine, but I'm not much on alcohol during the day. I hope you don't mind." Scott placed a glass bottle of water on the wall. Two cups and plates, napkins, a knife, and a lemon were the last items he added. "That about does it."

He twisted the bottle's cap and filled their cups. After cutting a lemon, he dropped a quarter in Isabella's cup and then handed it to her. "*Salute*. To Rome and to you, Miss Martini."

"*Salute*, Mr. Hancock. To Rome and to you, as well."

Isabella sipped the cool water. It delivered a chill behind her breastbone on its journey to her stomach. Far from dousing the fire that had begun burning within her, it added fuel to the flames. Was it Rome that made her feel as if she could fly, or was it Scott? Or both?

Scott cut off a slice of salami, then cheese, and placed them on the plate in front of Isabella. He held up the loaf of bread. "Do you prefer the end or middle?"

"Middle, please."

"Perfect. I prefer the end." Next, he sliced the egg in half and added one section to Isabella's plate. A look of unease graced his features. "I'm afraid I may have botched up. I took control of our lunch without thinking about your food preferences."

Isabella released a quick laugh. "I love food. All types of food. Except squid." She wrinkled her nose. "I draw the line at squid."

"We've no squid today, but I do enjoy fried calamari. Can you watch someone eat squid, or do you run screaming from the room?"

"No, I can stomach the sight. Just not the texture and the taste. I give you permission to eat it to your heart's content." Isabella inhaled a deep breath. The air was sweet and green, with the added pungent scents of the meat and cheese mixed in. "Tell me about this meal we're about to share. Is there a significance to it?"

"Glad you asked." Scott's plate contained the same assortment of food found on Isabella's. While he inserted his piece of salami and cheese into the heel of the bread loaf, he asked, "How well do you know ancient Roman Catholic traditions? Are you Catholic, by the way?"

Busy with her own sandwich preparation, Isabella shook her head. "I'm not Catholic. I do know a fair amount of the traditions but not ancient ones."

She tore her chunk of bread in two. She used the knife to slice her half of the egg into thin sections and then layered them on top of the salami and cheese. Next, she covered everything with the bread's other half and pressed down with the palm of her hand. She looked up to see Scott watching her.

"What? Am I doing it wrong?"

"Sorry. I'm enthralled. You've built your sarnie like a pro."

"Sarnie?"

"Sorry. Sandwich." Scott tapped Isabella's with his own. "*Buon appetito*!"

"*Grazie. Buon appetito*." She bit into the bread, closed her eyes, and chewed slowly.

The flavors were expected yet unexpected—sharp, tinged with paprika, and slightly acidic. The meat tasted as if it had been smoked over a wood fire. Hints of salt moved through her mouth as the cheese mixed with her saliva. Unlike the hard Romano cheese back home, this version was softer in texture and much more robust. Its creaminess bound all the flavors in a blanket of milky satin.

"Tell me, Isabella. Where does an American woman get a passion for simple Italian fare?"

"My mother and father would make a monthly journey to Boston. The North End, to be exact. When I got home from school, there would be a feast of meats and cheeses, and we would dine by making small sarnies, as you call them. We also had roasted red peppers, sardines, and a thick, peppery mustard… I was young, and I didn't like the sardines at all. Now I love them." She allowed her mind to travel back to those nights around the table. The three of them surrounded by joy and love. It felt wonderful to remember without any pain of melancholy.

Isabella brought her thoughts back to Rome. As before, Scott focused on her, his eyes reflecting the smile he wore.

Before she took another bite, she said, "You were going to tell me the significance of the food choices."

"Ah, yes. As I mentioned, my Mum used to take me here when I was a lad. We always had the same lunch. The story is the Mattei family, the original owners of this property, would open their doors on the day of the Visit of the Seven Churches. That's the day Romans would embark on a pilgrimage to visit the seven basilicas, a tradition started by Filippo Neri, in 1552. When they reached the Villa Mattei, they were given bread, wine, salami, cheese, an egg, and two apples, as well as access to the grounds on which they could rest before continuing their journey."

"Interesting. I take it you're Catholic? Have you completed the visits?"

"Yes. I attended parochial school here in Italy. Each Holy Thursday the students were bused to Rome and we'd set out with our heads bowed, giggling at whispered jollies instead of self-flagellating penance."

Isabella chuckled. "Were you one of the instigators?"

"Oh, yes, I didn't go in for all the chest beating. We were children. Not a lot of sinning under our belts just yet."

While talking, Scott cut one of the apples. He handed Isabella a section. "We need to eat one unless we won't have any good luck. I abhor the damn things, but it's custom."

"I love apples, so I'll eat most of it, and you can just nibble a tiny piece."

"Smashing. We have a perfect future together, Isabella Martini. I'll eat any calamari we encounter, and you can tackle the apples."

"Deal." Isabella licked a crumb from her bottom lip. "What's it like filming a love scene?"

"How do you mean?"

"Well, I wondered if… you know… do you…" Scott's eyebrows

shot up as Isabella choked out the question. "You know... get excited?"

"Right. You want to know if the little general salutes?"

"You call your, you know, the little general?"

"No, actually. I was trying to be polite. I'd much rather have you ask if I get an erection. You did mention that you had seen me naked. If you'd like, I can give you a peek."

Heat that had nothing to do with the hot weather flooded Isabella's cheeks. "Let's just drop this and forget I asked."

"Ah, buck up. Here, have some water before you combust." Chuckling, Scott twisted the cap off the water and filled her cup.

"Why do you seem to enjoy toying with me?" She chugged the water, nearly soaking her chin in the process.

"It's rather fun. Anyway, back to the topic at hand."

"No! Let's not go back."

Scott's laugh exploded. "I was going to say, it's not all that glamorous. There's camera and lighting blokes, the director is there yelling commands. *'Move your blooming hand to the left. Slower. Raise your leg!'* And then there's the makeup artists hovering with powder puffs. It's all rather distracting. However, you were about to ask if I get aroused." His grin took her by surprise with its implied bravado. "In truth, there are times one does get excited, in spite of the commotion. All I can do is apologize to whomever I'm with and hope the editing crew does their work. It wouldn't do to have my fan base disappointed."

"Oh, I'm sure your fans would be more than impressed." Isabella pressed her hands to her face and moaned. "I can't believe that just came out."

"I'm not. Thank you for your confidence in my prowess."

"You're welcome, and now may we please change the subject? Tell me about your next movie. What sort of character will you be playing?"

"A private investigator who has to retrieve a kidnapped girl from the wilds of Alaska. The rub is I've no survival skills, and she and I will have to fend for our lives while the bad guys try to kill us."

"They'll shoot the dangerous scenes in front of a green screen, won't they? I mean, they can't expect you to get all Leonardo like in *Revenant*."

"Actually, this director prefers realism, so we'll be shooting in the out of doors. Blizzards and all that. Sadly, my stunt double will get to have all the fun."

Isabella coughed a laugh. "You think running through the woods of Alaska will be fun. All you need is a few wolves chasing you, and then you'll change your tune."

"One can only hope. Anyway, it won't be all that bad. They have a lot invested in keeping the paid help alive."

Lost in thought as she chewed, Isabella wondered the age of the kidnapped character. He had said girl, so she must be young. Maybe twelve or, even better, ten.

"How old is the girl? The one who gets kidnapped?"

"I was wondering if you would ask." Scott bent and claimed his small piece of apple. "She's eighteen, but the actress is twenty-one, and yes, there'll be a sex scene. Two actually." He straightened and crunched a piece of apple. "Jealous?"

Isabella's narrowed eyes stared at him. "You really are full of yourself, Mr. Hancock. I don't know you well enough to be jealous."

She inserted a chunk of apple into her mouth.

"Well, just in case you are, you've nothing to worry about. I doubt if the actress wants to romp with a man three times her age. Besides—" He reached out and slid the back of his fingers along Isabella's cheek. "You seem to have stolen my heart."

A loud crunch escaped Isabella's mouth as she pressed her teeth into the apple.

Twenty-Five

SCOTT bellowed a laugh. "Well put."

Isabella almost choked. "I'm sorry. I had the piece in my mouth and didn't know what to do." She pressed her napkin to her lips and laughed.

"Fancy a walk? We can talk while I show you around."

"I'd love a walk."

Scott positioned the strap of Isabella's bag over his shoulder. In one hand he held the half-empty bottle of water. His other hand searched for Isabella's. She stepped forward, slid her fingers against his, and they began walking down a path that led deeper into the gardens. They stopped and chose a shady spot alongside a small, fenced-in pond.

"Are there always turtles in there?" Isabella watched the two dozen turtles pile on top of each other to attempt to be the uppermost and closest to the sun's rays.

Scott nodded. "Seem to come and go as they like."

They both settled back against the bench. A comfortable silence eased around them while the sounds of the park filled the air. Isabella reached for the water bottle. "Mind if I take a swig?"

"Have at it. When you're ready to talk, jump ahead."

"What makes you think I need to talk?"

"My comment about… you know… bugger all, I'm speaking dribble."

"No, you're not." Isabella drew a long drink, then handed the bottle to Scott. Although they sat in the shade and a breeze kept her cooled, Isabella felt the prickles of sweat piercing her skin. "I'm just not sure what to say."

"Then I'll start. Isabella, I'm the type of man who sees something he wants and takes it. Perhaps I've moved too fast for you. If so, I apologize." Scott took his fill of water and then continued. "I'm not asking you to plunge full ahead. But could you see me as a bloke you'd be willing to give a go? It won't be easy, I'll admit that. Being an actor is what I do; it's not who I am. However, the truth of the matter is I come with a basket of chaos. Can you run the course?"

Scott looked Isabella's way, an expression of expectancy creasing his handsome features.

Isabella took her cue. "I've spent over ten years cloistered by my own design. I've dated a bit...well, actually, the number of times could be counted out on one hand, but that's not the point. The point is no man seemed to want to get to know me, in part due to the walls I built. I have to admit, at first you rattled me. I couldn't understand why you, of all people, saw me as someone worth knowing."

She reclaimed the water bottle. "But you did. And I'm glad for it. I would be lying if I said I wasn't scared. However, it has nothing to do with your lifestyle, which is probably something I should be concerned about. I'm afraid of trusting someone again. And I'm fearful of trusting myself again. As you pointed out, I can leave destruction in my wake. I don't want to be hurt—and I don't want to hurt you. What if I disappoint you, like I did Freddy? I just don't want to travel down that rabbit hole again."

Isabella took a sip of water. Was it possible to step gingerly around the mines the relationship presented and not get blown to pieces?

"I can't make any guarantees I won't hurt you," Scott replied. "I'll most likely cause you many nights of sorrow."

"Oh, great. Thanks. Way to woo a girl." Isabella chuckled. "Pure poetry."

Scott joined her and added his own laugh. He put a hand on her hip and slid her close. He nuzzled the part of her hair that feathered along her temple. After planting a kiss, he said, "You are a cheeky crumpet, you know that?"

"So I've been told." She wanted to kiss him. Isabella turned her head and found his lips.

After a long pause, Isabella said, "I'm not able to make any promises. I'm just finding myself again. But I'm willing to give it a go, as you Brits are fond of saying."

Scott brought her hand up to his lips and kissed her palm. She placed her hand against his cheek and smiled at him. "One more thing. I ask that you understand I come with my own basket of chaos. Can you handle that, Mr. Hancock?"

"Yes, Miss Martini. I can handle that."

A man and woman with a trail of children walked up to the pond. What should have ended with a kiss took on a quiet moment of reflection. Scott and Isabella held hands and finished the bottle of water while the couple's children squealed at the turtles.

Glancing at his watch, Scott stood. "We best be going if we want to arrive before the boys."

While they walked back to the car, Scott explained the history behind the statuary they passed. Eventually arriving at the garden's entrance, he leaned against the car and pulled Isabella into his arms. His lips trailed along hers and the final pieces of her walls tumbled to dust.

"*Signora*, princess, I am finished with school." Michel burst onto the patio where Isabella sat.

"Congratulations, Michel. How wonderful." She scooped him into her arms and inhaled his childlike scent of sweat and powder. "I'll bet you're ready to burst with excitement."

"*Si*, I am to have a fun time. Tonight we will have pizza and see the lights."

Federico and Leonardo joined them, each wearing their own broad grins.

"We passed," Leonardo announced. "I am now one year away from the university."

Isabella released a cry of praise for both boys.

Scott came onto the patio, carrying a glass of sparkling water for Isabella. *"Ciao ragazzi. Come è stato il tuo ultimo giorno di scuola?"*

He grinned and added in English. "Sorry, Isabella. I asked how the last day of school was?"

Each boy took his turn giving the details of his day. When finished, they all chimed together about the night's celebration. Scott followed André's suit and forced the boys to slow down and take turns.

Michel went first. "We will have pizza."

"We will visit the Spanish Steps and have gelato," Federico added.

Leonardo finished with, "We will ride the train."

"Mia bambinos." André's voice called from inside the apartment, and the boys shot from the patio to greet her, leaving Scott and Isabella alone.

"They're like puppies," she laughed. "I'm not sure I can keep up with them tonight."

"You'll do splendidly." Scott slid his chair up to hers and cupped her chin. "I'll be there to carry you if you lose your footing."

His kiss took her breath away. The smooth way his mouth eased over her lips, teasing between them with his tongue, sent a series of delicious shivers throughout her body. She encircled his neck with her arms and melted into his desire.

"*Mam-ma. Zio* Scott and Princess, they are kissing." Michel's shout broke Scott and Isabella apart. Isabella knew instinctively that her face would be the color of the strawberries Luisa had served that morning.

André arrived wearing a knowing grin and winked at the two of them. "Are you corrupting my *bambinos?*"

"Sorry," Scott said. "It was bound to happen sooner or later. If you'll excuse me, I'll tend to the boys." He gave Isabella a quick kiss on her cheek and did the same to André. "Come, Michel, let's go for a walk and let the women have their time alone."

As soon as Scott and Michel left, André looked Isabella in the eyes. "Spill. I want all the glorious details."

Isabella started with the previous midnight meeting on the patio and then filled her in on the day's events.

"*Bravo*. My new friend and my dear Scott. We will have another reason to celebrate tonight."

"André, slow down. We're still working through the details."

"*Toro*! That's means 'bull' by the way. Details are for lawyers, not for matters of the heart. Do you love him?"

The question had been dogging Isabella throughout the day. Here it was. Voiced aloud, demanding an answer.

"I could."

"At least that's something. Now go put on another outfit, freshen your lipstick, and let's hit the town. Mario is meeting us at the Steps."

"But, André—"

"No buts! *Zitto*! Isabella, you've spent your life hidden away. Spread your wings and fly." André scooted Isabella from the patio. "*Andiamo*."

"Isabella." A soft knock preceded her name. "Are you awake?"

"Yes." Isabella stepped from the bed. "Come in," she murmured.

The door opened a crack, and Scott spoke into the room. "Meet me on the patio, if you don't mind."

"No, I don't mind. I'll be right out. Give me a minute."

Scott eased the door closed.

Isabella ran to the bathroom and quickly brushed her teeth. She slipped into her robe. Before leaving the room, she checked the time on her phone. Two o'clock!

The phone slipped from her hands, landing on the area rug with a soft thud. He's leaving. She didn't know where the thought came from, but it arrived with the force of a nor'easter. Every fiber of her bones shouted the realization. He's leaving Italy.

Scott stood by the fountain, his hands deep within his pants pockets, his eyes focused on the water. He had on a suit coat and tie.

When he saw her, he sprinted her way and took her in his arms. His mouth covered hers, delivering a force she had yet to receive. His arms formed an impenetrable fortress around her.

"Isabella, are you mine?"

"Yes, I'm yours."

She remained in his arms. He buried his lips against her neck. "Isabella, I'm sorry, I have to leave you."

He looked up and caught her face before she could turn away. A quick smile crossed his lips. "I knew you would pull away. Listen to me, lass. I have to fly to L.A. for a week or two. Something to do with the movie. I received a call a bit ago."

"Oh, okay." The familiar sensation washed over Isabella. "I see. No problem." She made to move back, but Scott shook his head.

"Don't pull away. Listen to me. I asked if you were mine, and you said yes. There's no going back."

"But... you're leaving. I don't see any point—"

"Don't say it. Don't." Scott's lips pressed his against hers.

Her hands gripped the lapel of his jacket. She returned his hunger, giving him years of longing and desire in the brief time they had.

But the tears wouldn't be consoled. They came in force, with a will of their own, and spilled down her face. "Scott, what if you don't come back?"

He kissed her eyes and cheeks, drying the salty flow with his lips.

"I'll return. You'll not be getting rid of me any time soon."

"Just leave." Isabella collapsed against his chest.

"Don't cry," Scott murmured. "It won't do a'tall for you to be red-eyed tomorrow. I want you to take Tuscany's breath away as you have mine."

Tears tightened Isabella's throat. "What if you change your mind?" She pushed him away. "Oh, that was a stupid thing to say." The tears flowed easily. "You're a grown man. If you want to change your mind... *ciao*, Scott." She turned and ran for the patio door.

"Isabella, stop." Scott reached her side and grabbed hold of her arm. "We'll not let the past cloud our future. I'll return. We'll spend two glorious weeks in Tuscany. I promise. But you. You must remain safe. Don't talk to strangers, minibus drivers, or give anyone your luggage. That reminds me..." He pulled out his phone. "What's your cell number? Do you still have the note I wrote you?"

"Oh, Scott, I never thanked you for the note! Yes, I still have it. It's in my ghastly bag." She tried to laugh, but couldn't find enough air in her lungs. It had all been sucked out by his news.

"Good. Call me if you need me. Now give me your number."

After Scott punched in her phone number, he returned his cell to his pocket. "Here is the number for my villa." He handed her a slip of paper.

Isabella took it, her tears dotting the surface with wet pools.

"There's a staff living there," he said. "I've instructed them to assist you if necessary. Should you have car trouble or you're too tired to drive, call them and they'll come to your aid. You're welcome to stay at my home until I return."

He bent low and kissed her again. "I would love to come back to find you in my bed." He kissed the base of her neck and inhaled. "There's so much of you I plan on discovering, and I want to watch you discover me. Fate will not take that away from us."

Trailing his mouth along her jaw, he found her lips again. His tongue drove into her mouth, a ravenous presence searching for its mate.

The arms around Isabella held her firm. Despite their strength, they couldn't hold back time.

"Bugger all, I've got to run or I'll miss my bloody plane. I will come back to you, Isabella. Have no doubt."

One last kiss, and then he left.

Isabella stood and listened. The sound of the car's engine roared into the distance.

She stood immersed in the floral scent of the patio and allowed the tears to flow as they wanted. As far as she was concerned, they could drown her.

The sorrow-filled night yielded to a morning alive with noise and succulent odors. Isabella heard the boys shouting and singing and André's calls for *silenzioso*. An assortment of aromas seeped into the room, starting with coffee and cinnamon. It called to Isabella to get out of bed and join the pandemonium.

She mentally scolded herself for becoming weepy and despondent. What made the chastising worse was the vision of the previous night and how she had latched onto Scott as if he were the only way she could pull herself from the quicksand of her past.

Scott couldn't do it for her. She had to free herself.

If Scott returned, she reasoned, she didn't want him to find her clinging to the past.

"Not if. When," she said. "He'll return. He promised." She wanted him to find her ready to embark on the future.

"I can do this. Heck, I've come this far; the rest should be a piece of cake."

Whispers and soft giggles leaked under the door. Isabella chuckled and slid from under the bed covers. Silently moving to the door, she slowly twisted the knob. With a quick pull, she yanked it open and shouted, "*Buongiorno*!"

A stampede of laughter careened into her, carrying her back onto the bed.

She tickled and hugged the boys, relishing the joy they brought with them. This was a much better way to start the day.

After she kissed each boy in turn, she announced, “I need coffee!”

They spilled from the room. Swooping into the kitchen, they descended on André and Luisa.

The End

Epilogue

THE Hertz attendant parked the Audi A4. After assisting Isabella with her luggage, he reviewed the car's features and GPS system.

"If you want to change your destination, this is the way you must do it."

"I want to drive up the Amalfi Coast. Can we make the system take me along that route?" she asked, still marveling at her brazenness at renting a convertible.

"*Si, Signora.* This we can do."

"*Grazie.*"

In less than sixty seconds, Isabella started the car and pulled out of the rental lot.

"Here goes nothing."

Her grip on the steering wheel tightened as she headed for *via Leone Delagrange*, the first major roadway she would drive on alone.

Scott's original advice played in her head. 'Just stay on the right and ignore the other drivers.'

"How can I ignore the other drivers when all they're doing is honking at me?" She'd asked André.

André's guidance had been the same as Scott's. 'Stay to the right.' Only she had added, 'Listen to some music and wear this hat and scarf. You'll look like Gina Lollobrigida.'

Instead of focusing on her potential death, Isabella thought over the text she'd received.

Farfella. We just flew over the bottom tip of Greenland. Halfway to L.A. I'll return to you. On that you can depend. It might be too soon to text I love you but I'll think it. Caio, Mr. Hancock.

"Not too soon, Mr. Hancock. Perhaps it's not too soon at all."

Isabella smiled and pressed the power button for the radio.

Music blended with the blaring horns of traffic as she pulled onto the *Autostrada* and began the second part of her Italian adventure.

Dear Reader,

I hope you enjoyed the first installment in Isabella's Story. Perhaps you'd like to read *The Summer of Annah: A Midsummer's Wish*, available at Amazon in electronic and paperback formats. I hope you will. And, I'd be grateful if you'd leave a review on Amazon or Goodreads (*grazie*).

Blessed be,

Cinthia

About Tinthia

Tinthia Clemant lives on the Concord River with a rescue Sheltie, elderly cat, rabbits, flock of wild Mallards, and assorted songbirds, turtles, and snakes. As a compelling new voice in woman's fiction, she believes in the power all women possess to take hold of their destinies and direct their fates. She also believes in the power of ice cream, chocolate, and being true to one's dreams.

She loves to hear from fans and can be reached at tinthia@tinthia-clemant.com. Follow her on Twitter, Youtube, Google+, Pinterest and Goodreads.

www.ingramcontent.com/pod-product-compliance
Lightning Source LLC
Chambersburg PA
CBHW022102170626
?08CB00002B/553